S P Y

By

Harold Fischel

This book is a work of fiction. Names, characters, places, and incidents either are products of the author's imagination or are used fictitiously.

Any resemblance to actual persons, living or dead, events, or locales is
entirely coincidental.

ISBN: 978-0-578-41256-6 (print & ebook)

PART ONE

Matt

Chapter One

Pungent smoke burned his nostrils as he gazed at the rubble that minutes before had been his office. He had just returned from a meeting with General Edelman. During the drive back to the secure compound they called Centri 4, he received a warning that the compound was under attack by ISIS. He told his driver to speed up. They flew through the main gate which had been reduced to a smoldering heap of rubble. When they reached his office building the intense firefight was over. The attacking rebels were dead. Ambulances with screaming sirens arrived and medics started searching among the rubble in hopes of finding survivors. All he could do was watch as the bodies of five of his men were recovered and loaded into an ambulance like cordwood. The chief medical officer came over and informed him that the remains of the other members of his staff had been located but were so mutilated that they would have to be recovered by a special team.

Major Mathaeus (Matt) Ramsey returned to his vehicle. He looked for his driver. At first he could not locate him. After a short search Matt found the young private hunched over between two buildings. He had been sick to his stomach and was crying. Matt knew that Billy Daniels had just arrived from the U.S and had not seen combat before. He went over and put his arm around the young soldier's shoulders. Slowly he walked Billy back to the jeep and loaded the youngster into the passenger seat. Matt got behind the wheel and drove over to Headquarters Troop with jaws clinched tight.

Master Sergeant Martinez was in the dayroom when Matt escorted Billy in. "Sarge, Billy was with me when I inspected the remains of HQ and he saw the bodies being carried out. Please take care of him." Without waiting for the sergeant's response Matt turned around and left. He returned the jeep to the motor pool, retrieved his car and drove directly to Lagoon Bar located downtown right along the river. The bar was crowded with locals discussing the ISIS assault on the military base which the Americans shared with the Kurdish Peshmerga. Matt found a seat at the bar and ordered a shot of scotch. "Make that a double," he threw in as an afterthought.

When he took his first greedy swallow of scotch Matt heard a female voice coming from his left. "Major that scotch is too good to gulp down like that. Take it easy and enjoy it."

Matt turned to his left and looked at the smiling face of a woman sitting next to him. She was dressed in dark green old-fashioned fatigues. "How did you know I'm in the military?" he asked.

"Major Ramsay you're still wearing your uniform and I can see your rank and name. You're not supposed to wear your uniform in downtown Irbil and certainly not when drinking in a bar. So I suppose you're very shook-up about the ISIS attack on your base."

Matt stared at the woman. *Who the hell is she and what does she want with me?* The fatigues and cap she was wearing looked like old leftovers from the East German army. Under the cap her hair was tightly drawn back into a large bun. Her features were definitely not Iraqi or Kurdish. He could only guess at her age. Matt was curious about who this dame could be. Judging by her accent she was definitely not American. He couldn't place her accent but it sounded sexy.

He decided on a non-committal response to her approach. "Sorry, I don't recall meeting you but do I know you?"

"Not likely. I have seen you before, here in the Lagoon. I don't think you noticed me."

"Your uniform has no markings."

She laughed. "It's not a uniform. I wear this outfit when I'm out in the field. You're right it has no markings. But to be fair, since I know your name and that you're in the US army I'll show you my I.D. badge." She pulled out a small plasticized I.D. and laid it on the bar in front of Matt. He looked at it and read:

IEDC
International
Engineering Design and
Construction
Senior Project Manager
Helga Kozlov, Ph.D

"We're in the process of restoring a hydroelectric power plant along the River Zab near Makhmour. ISIS wants to disable the power station located on the river. They make almost daily attempts to infiltrate through the Kurdish lines which are strung out along the river. So I'm no stranger to attacks by those bastards. Were you on base when they made that surprise attack today?"

"No I wasn't."

"Oh, what's your job here in Irbil?"

"I check the quality of the ice cream served in the PX."

Helga laughed and the serious look disappeared from her face. "Okay, I should have known better than to ask. I'm sorry! But there is no rule that you have to drink alone. Bartender, please give me a Vodka Sour and give my friend here a refill."

Matt found her somewhat forward but saw no harm in talking to her. She seemed friendly enough. "You're over here to inspect the work at the dam?"

"No such luck. That project is my baby. I live here in Irbil and will be stuck here until the Peshmerga fully control the area here and around Mosul. As long as there is concern that ISIS fighters break through the lines and attack the dam, my assignment will be to stay put."

"So you live here. Interesting. What does a foreigner like you, a woman, do for entertainment here in Irbil?"

"Read books, lots of books. Sometimes I come here looking for someone to talk to."

"Don't you have any friends here in town?"

"Woo. That's a lot of questions coming from a guy who can't even tell me what he does."

"Fine! Okay, so I won't ask. I respect that. You're Helga and we'll leave it at that."

"Hey, I didn't mean it that way. No I don't have any friends here in town. All the foreign nationals hightailed it out of here when ISIS advanced within thirty miles. The locals are nice to me, but I get tired of hearing how this war has ruined life here in the Kurdish capitol, Erbil as the international press calls it. Did you see this newspaper article?" Helga showed Matt an article in an old newspaper she pulled from her purse.

Yesterday President Obama authorized the use of air strikes in Iraq— if the terror group ISIS moved on the Iraqi city of Irbil. Early this morning, the bombs started falling, "the first offensive action by the US in Iraq since it withdrew ground troops in 2011," says the Guardian.

This morning two F/A-18 fighter jets bombed ISIS artillery that was advancing on Irbil. The city of 1.6 million, also known as Arbil or Erbil and as *Hewlêr* in the local Kurdish language is the regional capital of Iraqi Kurdistan, an autonomously governed region in northeastern Iraq.

Just a few months ago Irbil was seen as a safe haven from ISIS' incursions into Iraq, and the city and the surrounding region have been swarmed by refugees. Irbil is also the temporary home to American troops and advisers sent to Iraq to help with the ISIS incursion, and the site of the U.S. consulate in Iraqi Kurdistan.

Yet modern military targets are not the only thing in Irbil worth protecting. Irbil is, according to the United Nations, among "the oldest continuously inhabited human settlements in the world." The city has been touched by ancient civilizations, says the U.N., "such as the Sumerian, Babylonian, Greek, Islamic, and Ottoman." The massive citadel at the heart of the city was added to the U.N.'s World Heritage list not even two months ago.

Irbil is "a layer cake of civilizations that have come and gone for an estimated 7,000 to 10,000 years," says the New York Times. The city has seen continuous occupancy since 5,000 B.C., though its history "might go back further," said an archaeologist to the Times. Archaeological digs within the city have turned up human bones that are 7,000 years old.

For the most part Irbil has been able to stay out of the fray for most of the past seven years. Now, as ISIS continues to expand the territory it controls in the Middle East, it is right in the middle.

It's a sad story for the region. Just a few years ago local leaders were talking about how to drive tourism

"What about the folks in your company? Don't you hang around with them?"

"Come on, as an army officer you know damn well that you don't get too palsy-walsy with the people you supervise. I'm their boss and I have to prevent any of the guys getting too romantic with me."

"If you don't mind me saying so, that sounds a little conceited."

"Okay, I get it. Sorry I bothered you. Just trying to make some small talk." Helga got up and started to move away.

As she slid off the bar stool Matt reached over and stopped her. "You're right. I'm acting like an ass. I'm upset. That ISIS attack today; my men got killed." Helga turned to face him and Matt continued, "If I apologize will you sit down and finish your drink?"

Helga got back onto the bar stool. "I guess a bad beginning is better than no beginning. I just wanted to talk to someone, and sitting next to a handsome soldier seemed like a good opportunity."

"Let *me* start this time. Hi, I'm Matt and I wouldn't mind taking to this nice lady sitting next to me."

That made for a much better start and when the bartender announced last call they were still deeply engrossed in conversation. All through the evening they kept the liquor flowing, ignoring the bartender's gentle warning to take it easy. Not too long after last call the bartender approached them. "Major, Madame, I'm sorry, but we're closing and I have to ask you to leave."

Matt reached for his keys. "I hope I can remember where I parked my car. I'll give you a lift home when we find it." He slurred his words and wobbled on his feet when he got up. Helga was clearly quite tipsy but in better shape than Matt.

"No way. You're in no condition to drive." She grabbed his keys away from him. "Bartender please call a taxi." Matt objected. "At this time of night they won't allow a taxi on the base."

"Don't worry, I'll take care of that." Helga took him by the arm and gently led him outside. Moments later their taxi arrived.

Chapter Two

The noise coming from the street below woke him. He felt something leaning on his chest and when he opened his eyes he saw a woman was lying next to him with her arm slung over him. It took Matt a moment to realize who it was. "Oh shit Helga! What the hell, where am I?"

Helga woke with a start. She sat up and smiled at Matt. "Calm down, honey. It's okay, we're in my apartment."

"Your apartment? How did we get here and … " Matt pushed himself to a sitting position. "How did we get into this bed?"

Helga burst out laughing. "Well, I must say worse things could happen to you!"

Matt jumped out of the bed but when he realized he was wearing nothing but his underwear he grabbed the sheet to cover himself. By doing that he left Helga uncovered and to his consternation she was only in her bra and panties.

Helga continued laughing; she found the whole thing hilarious. "Don't worry; my parents are not home." When she stopped laughing she said, "Just joking. I love the shocked look on your face and the way you turned red when you saw I was half naked. You're obviously a respectable man Major Matt. Seriously, we were sauced when we left the bar. I could not let you drive so I called for a taxi. You were sober enough to tell me that a taxi would not be allowed on base that late. So, I told the taxi to take us here to my apartment."

Matt looked questioningly at Helga. "Did we . . . ?"

"Nope. You were the perfect gentlemen. You did not try to take advantage of this drunken lady! I was perfectly safe; you couldn't have done anything if you'd wanted to; you were much too drunk. The taxi driver helped drag you up here to my apartment. As soon as we put you on the couch you fell asleep. I did not want you waking up stiff as a board in a rumpled uniform. I managed to get you over to my bed and I removed your uniform. I went to undress and get ready for bed myself, but I heard you groan and I went to check on you. With all that liquor we drank I must have been pretty far gone too and I passed out on top of you."

"If I was in your bed where were you planning to sleep?"

"Wouldn't you like to know? Sorry sweetie, that will remain a secret. But stop worrying. There was no sex, and as far as I know, you did not even get to touch me. Actually, I think I was the one hugging you. Now get in the bathroom and take a quick shower. While you're dressing I'll make us breakfast."

Matt dropped the sheet. With Helga standing there in her panties and bra he felt a little foolish covering himself with the sheet. He looked at Helga. She looked different from the woman in fatigues with her hair in a bun under a uniform cap. Freed from the bun, her long blond hair fell freely across her shoulders. With her bright misty green/ blue eyes, round face, full cheeks and high forehead

Matt thought she looked captivatingly Slavic. He was sorry that last night he had failed to ask where she was from.

Helga caught him staring at her body. The tight bikini panties accentuated her strong athletic thighs and firm belly. Coyly she asked, "Well, do you approve?"

"Yes, very nice." Matt relaxed a little and laughed at her seeking approval of her body which she obviously kept in shape.

Helga returned the compliment. "You're not so bad yourself. Do you like to work out?"

"Yeah, I would if we had some exercise facility on the base."

"Go look in the room next to the kitchen."

Matt forgot that he was walking around in his underwear and went to look. Helga followed closely. She was anxious to hear what he thought about her well-equipped gym. The room next to the kitchen was filled with exercise equipment. The obvious quality surprised Matt. "Hey, you have a professional gym in here."

"Yes, I'm addicted to my daily workout. I imported all this equipment from America. When it arrived, the Iraqi government impounded it. I had a hell of a time explaining why I needed it. I showed them the mail-order magazine I ordered the stuff from. It was advertised as commercial quality adapted for home use. They were impressed with how expensive the equipment was. You're more than welcome to come over some time and use it."

Helga noticed Matt was paying more attention to her breasts than the exercise equipment. "Yoo-hoo! I invited you to use the exercise equipment. Not to come play with my boobs."

"Yeah beautiful equipment," Matt said while he continued to admire her breasts which were pushing out of the top of her bra exposing most of what she had.

Helga clearly enjoyed the attention her breasts were getting but decided to cool things down when she saw movement in Matt's briefs. "Too soon for that! Now be a good boy and go and take a shower. Your uniform is hanging in my closet. By the way, I noticed the scars on your side. Did you get hurt in the army?"

"Yeah I got wounded while serving in Afghanistan. No big deal. Some flesh wounds that's all."

Matt dressed himself in the bathroom and when he entered the kitchen he was surprised to find Helga also already fully dressed. "Sit down; I made you some fried eggs. I left them in the pan, and they're pretty well done. I hope you like them that way."

"That's great thanks." Helga didn't look anything like the well-built sexy woman who sent him to take a shower. "How come you wear fatigues?"

"I work in a war zone; remember the dam is under constant attack."

Matt sat down at the kitchen table. Helga had prepared a full breakfast and poured him a cup of coffee. "Aren't you afraid ISIS will overrun that place and take control of the dam?"

"Not really. I have great faith in the Peshmerga. They have to hold the dam; it's important to this whole area. But you never know; things could go wrong. I'm used to it. My company only works in troubled areas. Oil fields, pipe lines, you name it - when there is fighting going on they call in IEDC to keep installations going and to fix any damage."

Matt glanced at his watch. "It's getting late, I better get back. When I left last night I called the colonel and told him I was heading to town to have a drink. I don't want him wondering what happened to me; I'm required to let him know at all times where I am."

Helga was disappointed. "I was hoping you could stay a little longer, so we could chat some more. I really enjoyed talking to you last night. I've felt rather isolated since the foreigners pulled out of here. I already called my crew chief and told him I would not be at the dam until this afternoon. Too bad, I'll call a taxi to take you to your car."

Matt got up and waited for Helga to let him out. At the door he turned to her, "Can I kiss you goodbye?"

Helga hesitated before answering. "I think a hug will do." Matt had expected more and was not too happy with her answer. That quickly changed when she put both arms around his neck and gave him a tight embrace. Her lips brushed against his ear when she said, "You forgot to ask for my phone number. I need a friend in this town. Or was this our version of a one-night stand?"

Relieved that he was not getting a brush off Matt hugged her back. "Not on your life. You're not getting rid of me that fast. Let me write that number down so I don't forget. In case you haven't noticed, I like you and I too could use a friend, a female friend. I like you a lot! Let me give you my personal cell phone; my military phone is just for official business. Actually, it's a court martial offense to use it for personal calls. That's a pain because calls from my personal phone go through the US over and back."

"I have no such problem. Since I use it worldwide, the company supplies me with an iridium phone. It goes via satellite and I can use it everywhere for voice and text." She pulled one of her business cards from her pocket and pointed to the phone number.

Matt had no trouble finding his car; it was parked half a block from the club entrance. He hurried back to the post and went to the colonel's office which was in the undamaged part of the bombed building.

At first the colonel did not seem interested where he had been. "Matt get yourself ready. You're accompanying the bodies of your men to Dover Airforce base. Helicopters will fly you out of here to Irbil Airport and from there you'll fly directly to Dover."

"Yes sir! I'm on my way."

Matt turned to leave the office, but the colonel stopped him. "I know you were upset yesterday and rightly so but I could have used you here. Sergeant Major Coons had to make all the arrangements to fly the bodies back. I did not call you back in, but you should have been supervising that."

"Sorry sir. Fred, we've served together for a long time and you know I don't duck out when needed; but during this tour here I got a little too close to those men. It was selfish of me to leave. I'm sorry sir or Fred or whatever you want me to call you when you're pissed off at me."

"Matt nobody is pissed off. You just needed to take a deep breath, and I think you felt guilty that you were not there to defend them. Well, let me tell you there was nothing you could have done. They snuck onto our post and detonated those bombs before any of us could step in. I'm glad you weren't on post at the time, you'd probably be dead. But I'm curious, where the hell did you hang out all night and still look so fresh?"

"I met a nice lady in the bar at the Lagoon. She made sure I did not drive back, I was pretty much under the weather."

"Good for her! Did you catch her name?"

"Yeah, she's Helga Kozlov."

"I know her. Pretty exclusive company you were in. Did you know she is in charge of the IEDC crew over at the hydroelectric dam? You might be a little out of your league playing around with a dame like that."

"It's not what you think. We're just friends."

"Just keep in mind, for the Peshmerga in this area she carries the same weight as a US general."

Chapter Three

Matt's cell phone rang. It wasn't the military one, so he did not bother to answer. Probably one of those pesky robot calls about credit card rates. When it rang for the second time he picked it up intending to tell them to get the hell of his line. "Matt it's me Helga!"

"Hold on one second." He turned to the colonel. "Fred, will you excuse me for a moment while I take this call?" The colonel waved okay with his hand and Matt stepped into the hallway.

"Hi there. I just got back and meant to call you as soon as I had a free moment."

"Oh, I was wondering if you'd lost my number or maybe you didn't mean it when you said you wanted to see me again."

"Are you kidding? I'm dying to see you again, but the trip to Dover took longer than expected. I accompanied the caskets of the men who died in the bombing here at the barracks. As their commander I met with most of the families who came to Dover. Can I call you back in a while? I'm talking to my colonel right now."

"Sure, but how about coming over and using my gym. After those long plane rides back and forth to the States I'm sure you can use a workout."

"Sounds great. When?

"I thought you said you wanted to see me. What's wrong with tonight?"

"Deal! I'll be there as soon as I close up shop here."

When Matt went back into the colonel's office Fred said, "May I assume that was your new lady friend?"

"Yeah, that was Helga."

"I don't think it's here nor there, but you do know she is a Russian national don't you?"

"No, I didn't. What are you trying to tell me?"

"Nothing really, but military intelligence here in Iraq can get kind of shitty about such things. In her case there should be no problem. IEDC is a well-known American company. Their offices are located in Austin, Texas. They worked with us when we had all those oil wells on fire during the war. Helga is a big deal in IEDC. I'm told she is a brilliant engineer and gets sent out on the most difficult projects. I'm sure you won't have a problem; she has been a US resident for a long time, and she's had free access to our military bases during the war."

"Thanks for cluing me in. My father immigrated from Hungary, so we'll have some more to talk about."

Fred burst out laughing. "Get off it. Sure, a good friend and something to talk about. Who do you think you're kidding? She is one hell of a beautiful dame who hides behind a set of outdated fatigues. If I were twenty years younger I'd be chasing her myself."

Matt smiled and calmly continued briefing the colonel about new instructions he brought back from the States.

Chapter Four

They had been showing off for each other and were dripping in sweat when they finally quit. "For a guy who claims not to work out you're in pretty damn good shape."

Matt wiped his forehead. "I had a hell of a time keeping up with you. Wow! That was rough!"

"You're in no shape to get dressed that way. Go to my room and get into the shower."

Matt did not object. He was exhausted, and a quick shower would feel good. When he stepped out of the shower and grabbed the clean towel Helga had laid out for him, Helga came into the bathroom. She took the towel from him and started to dry his back. When she had toweled off most of him she said, "Okay, go finish drying in the bedroom. My turn in the shower." She handed him the towel and stepped out of her training pants before disappearing behind the glass shower door. Matt was left staring awkwardly after her. He was embarrassed; his penis showed her touch had aroused him. He did not know what to make of this woman. *Is she playing with me or does she have other things in mind?* Matt finished dressing and went into the living room to wait for Helga. When she joined him, he suggested they go have dinner at a restaurant called Marina in nearby Ainkawa. Helga was not familiar with that restaurant.

That surprised Matt and she explained, "I told you I don't have any friends and a single gal doesn't go to a fancy restaurant by herself."

Matt filled her in about the restaurant he wanted to take her to. "I think it's the only restaurant in the province that stocks some great French wines and has only English-speaking waiters."

A few days after their dinner date Matt learned about another side of Helga. The sirens on the post sounded loudly with that high pitch Matt hated. At the same time his military phone barked the order for him to join a Peshmerga unit which was moving out to reinforce the troops guarding the dam. His standing instructions were not to join the fighting but have his unit accompany the Peshmerga fighters as advisors.

He was sitting in the passenger seat of an old half-ton truck driven by Ammar his Iraqi translator. When they approached the dam, they saw that a heavy firefight was taking place around the administration building. Matt's first thought was, *Helga is in there.*

"Ammar, quick get me over there!"

"Major you don't even have a weapon. Let the Peshmerga go in first."

Matt reminded Ammar that they carried weapons in back of all trucks. "You carry a bunch of M3 automatic machineguns in back of this truck. We'll use those old grease guns to help push ISIS back. Step on it we've got to get whoever is in that building out of there."

Ammar drove right up to the back of the building and the two of them raced in carrying two M3s each loaded with thirty round clips. In the back hall they encountered a bunch of ISIS fighters. Without hesitating they gunned them down. They stepped over the bodies and headed for the front offices. Carefully they pushed open the door to the main office, but the room was empty. They turned to inspect the next office, but as they reentered the hallway, a burst of automatic fire came from the far end. Three ISIS rebels who had been stalking them lay sprawled in a pool of their own blood. Helga emerged from the small room in the back carrying a Colt AR-15 carbine.

"You boys should be more careful. Those three suckers were right behind you when you entered the office."

"We never saw them. Did you watch us from the time we entered the building?" Matt asked.

"No. I hid in the back room when ISIS broke through our perimeter and started searching through this building. I'm afraid they got some people in the front room. Let's go see."

When they entered the front office what they encountered was horrible. Spread around the office were the bodies of at least ten Kurdish soldiers. Among the bodies Helga identified three of her IEDC crew. Helga went over to check if she could see some signs of life. To no avail, all three had multiple gunshot wounds. Sadly she turned to Matt. "Most of my crew got out before ISIS reached the building; I went back in to see if I could bring these three to safety. When I saw I was too late I ducked into the back room. You two arrived just in time; they were just about to check out the back room."

Ammar went outside to survey the surrounding area. When he returned he said to Helga, "I'm glad we got here before they found you in the back room. You returned the favor and mowed them down before they got us. From the fading sound of gunfire and explosives, I think our reinforcements have driven the rebels back. By now they must have cleared the zone around the dam and the area around this building is safe."

Matt agreed with Ammar that the rebels had probably been repelled, and he was ready to go outside and check on his men who had been dispersed among the Peshmerga. Helga was anxious to rejoin her crew. Outside they met Agrin Sivan the Kurdish commander.

Agrin explained, "Only a small group attacked this site. They never intended to take the dam. It was a diversionary tactic. We took a couple of prisoners and they gladly (he let out a thunderous laugh) told us about the ISIS plan to attack the city of Irbil. I have to get my men in position to defend the main highway to the city. But I have been ordered to first escort all IEDC people to our base where they'll be safe. The road back home to Irbil will be too dangerous for them. Don't worry, it won't take my men long to chase those bastards all the way back to Mosul. And we Kurds will take back Mosul. I promise!"

Helga was annoyed. "What's with this *my men?!* More than a third of your fighters are women."

"That's right Madam Director. We have a lot of women fighters. They fight like men; maybe even better. So I call all my troops men. They're tough like you, Madam. By the way, my headquarters called and they named you by name. The first thing they wanted to know if you were okay, and then they instructed me to bring you safely back to the base."

To accommodate the IEDC crew on base involved a little shoveling around of rooms but eventually a suitable place was found for everybody. Matt volunteered his Bachelor Officers Quarters (BOQ) room for Helga, but that became a little complicated when the colonel informed him he would not be embedded with the Kurds during their mission to clear the road to Irbil. Helga did not make a problem of it. "Hell, we shared a room before and survived it."

Matt's BOQ room was just that. A small room that contained a bed, a chair and a table that served as his desk. The bathroom was down the hall. Helga looked around. "It's not the Ritz-Carlton, but it is better than getting shot at on the way to my place."

They sat around talking for a long time. Helga seated on the bed and Matt in the chair. He apologized for not having any food or drink to offer her. "The mess hall, or what we like to call the mess hall, is closed and we don't allow liquor on the base anyway."

"We drank enough in the Lagoon to last us quite a while, and we don't need liquor for what I'm thinking."

"What's that?"

"Both of us almost got killed today and that should be a signal for me to finally make up my mind. You never know when something could happen to one of us, and then it would be too late."

"I'm not following, what do you mean by that?"

"This bed might be smaller than mine, but it's big enough for what I'm planning. Come on take off your clothes."

"Are you serious or are you playing one of your games?"

While she started to strip off her clothes Helga said, "Believe it or not, I was never playing a game. I was testing myself; I had to know if I was ready."

That confused Matt even more. "Testing yourself? What on earth for?"

"Are we going to spend all night talking about it or what? Or don't you want to have sex with me?" Helga did not wait for his response. She pulled Matt over to the bed and started tugging at his clothes. When they were both naked she pushed him onto the bed and fell on top of him. Matt eagerly responded and as their bodies pressed together their hands roamed around groping any part they could reach. They relished the feel of each other and it took a while before she carefully guided him into position as she whispered, "Go slow, I want you but I'm scared it will hurt."

Matt didn't fully understand but despite his full state of arousal he entered her very gently. After they were both spent, Helga snuggled up to Matt and they fell asleep.

Helga woke up before dawn and her movement woke up Matt. She sat up and said to Matt, "You're the first man I have ever willingly had sex with."

"You mean you were forced before?"

"You're a great guy, so I know you won't hold it against me. I'll explain but I warn you it's not a pretty story. Sit up next to me, and I'll tell you everything."

Matt sat up with his head leaning against the backboard. Helga snuggled next to him. "Hold me tight so I have enough courage to tell you what happened to me a long time ago back in Russia." Helga pulled the sheet up to cover their legs and started. "At a girls' boarding school I was raped by the gym instructor. I was in eighth grade, and no matter how I fought I could not hold him off me. I wildly flayed my arms and tried to kick him but I could not get away. He held me down and ripped my vagina when he brutally forced his penis in me. He hurt me terribly. When I ran back to my room my roommate noticed immediately that I was bleeding from my vagina. I was crying hysterically but managed to tell her what happened. She got out one of her sex-toys and helped me douche repeatedly with hot water and strong green soap.

"We did not tell anybody the gym instructor had raped me for fear we would be kicked out of school if he claimed I had tried to seduce him; he could have said I inflicted the wounds on myself because he rejected my advances. After all my father had to do to get me into that famous school, there was no way I could leave. When my mother was dying she made my father promise he would get me the best possible education. To do that he joined the communist party and used the connections he made in the party to have me admitted to the school.

"My roommate made sure I was protected from further assaults by that man. Her father was a big brute of a man, and she told the gym teacher if he ever came near me again her father would find him and beat the crap out of him.

"When we graduated from the boarding school my roommate and I went to the same university. Again, we roomed together because slowly but surely she had made me into her lover. After we graduated from the university, we lived together in an apartment in Paris. I attended the Ecole Normale Superieure, ENS. By that time my roommate was already a pretty successful artist. When she discovered I did not really love her but went along out of gratitude for what she had done for me in boarding school, she kicked me out. I did not have the slightest clue she was already having an affair with the lady who owned the apartment we were living in. I graduated from ENS with high honors and was accepted at MIT. I received my master's degree in engineering and switched to Texas A&M to enroll in their Doctor of Engineering (D.E.) program.

"I was desperately afraid of any close relationship with men, and I had no romantic feelings for women. So, I stayed away from any romance and definitely from sex. I concentrated on my education; after receiving my D.E.in engineering I stayed in Texas, went to work for IEDC. My career has been everything for me.

"That is until a guy named Major Ramsey entered my life. It started out rather innocently. I was lonely and wanted to talk to someone. As usual I was wearing that ill-fitting camouflage outfit of mine to prevent any man from getting any sexual ideas. We got into a great conversation. He told me about the young corporal killed during the ISIS attack. She blossomed and became much more assertive after he told me about arranging for his staff sergeant, who made a female worker uncomfortable with his remarks filled with sexual innuendo, to be transferred back to the US. Clearly, he did not tolerate men who harassed the women in his outfit. During the evening we drank too much. I really liked the guy. I had nothing to fear from him and felt comfortable talking to him, so I wasn't about to let him kill himself on the road back to his base. I took him to my apartment and somehow fell asleep in his arms. When I woke up I felt great. I had to admit to myself that it felt very nice sleeping in his arms.

"Things started really happening when we got up. I was half naked, and instead of trying to take advantage of me, like I assumed most men would, he was embarrassed. He was so cute standing there with that red blush on his face that I felt a slight tug in my heart. That was something I had never experienced before. As a distraction, I showed him my gym. I could not help it but my breasts were busting out of my bra. I saw him react and I was afraid he would try to grab me. But he didn't. I played a little coy to see if he really would respect me and treat me as a friend or turn on me and do what I expected from men. He didn't; I didn't feel threatened by this guy and really hoped to see him again. I feared my actions might have put him off a little, so when he was leaving I made it very clear our relationship could go further. When he was gone a couple of days on a trip to the US, I admitted to myself that I missed him. I surprised myself and called him. You have no idea how happy I was that he was eager to see me. That night I really tested myself. Would I feel comfortable touching his naked body? Could I trust him to let me set the boundaries as to how far I wanted to go?

"Sounds crazy but I had not seen a man's penis since that horrible incident at the boarding school. I looked at his erect penis, and it did not scare me like it had long ago. I realized I was falling in love with Major Ramsey. And tonight I really wanted you. But I was scared. The gym teacher at the boarding school hurt me badly and at times I wake up in a cold sweat reliving the experience. I had to overcome my fear. Luckily, my instincts about you were right. You were as eager as I, but you treated me very gently. You even waited for me to take hold of your penis to guide you in. It did not hurt; it felt great."

Helga reached up and kissed Matt. "Darling I'm really in love. Me in love with a man! I'm a girl, a real girl with girly feelings. I no longer worry what I am. I'm a girl! Do you understand what that means; how unbelievable happy I am that tonight was so great?"

Matt reached over and held her tight. He gently stroked her breasts and her nipples hardened. Helga rested her hand on his thigh and when she felt him respond she rolled on top of him. She did not mind that he was not as gentle with her as the night before; she loved the greedy way he entered her.

Totally exhausted they lay quietly for a while. Helga savored the weight of Matt's large frame on top of her. Matt was the first to speak. "I don't know how it could happen so fast but I love you, too, Helga, and I think I understand how you feel."

"Do you mind that I had sex with a woman?"

"Sweetheart, I'm crazy about you and my heart aches hearing about what you had to endure. I hope I can help you forget all that. Just be my gal forever and I promise to be your guy." Matt paused and a frown crossed his brow. "Talking
about forever, in our excitement last night we didn't take precautions. Even if I had thought of it I don't own any condoms."

Helga put his mind at ease. "Tonight did not come as a sudden impulse, and I have been taking the pill for a while. After that first night we met I knew you were special. So, just in case, I bought contraceptive pills. I have taken them long enough so we're safe."

Matt burst out laughing. "That's hilarious. If I had only known I would not have been so worried that this beautiful woman was playing with me."

"To help me forget what happened at that school there is something you can do. Before my mom died they called me Dorogaya. That means sweetheart. I was a happy kid, but not very verbal. I pronounced it Oraya and it stuck as my pet name. Would you mind calling me Oraya? That would remind me of those happy times. With you in my life happy times have come back. *Ya lyublyu tebya.*"

Matt smiled. "Oraya I can handle but what does that last part mean?"

"That's Russian for I love you. Don't worry you don't have to go that far. As long as you keep telling me in English that you love me, my world is complete."

Matt glanced at the clock. "Four-twenty, too early to get up. Let's go back to sleep for a while."

"Okay." Helga slid back under the sheet and snuggled once more against Matt. She whispered, "I love you darling," as she dozed off.

Chapter Five

Tightly curled in each other's arm they were still fast asleep when Matt's military phone started beeping. He reached over to pick it up. "Major Ramsay speaking, sir." He listened intently for a while and hung up. "That was the colonel. He wants me in his office as soon as possible."

Helga was disappointed. "Oh damn. Can't we lie here just a little while longer? I'm not ready to give you up."

"Oraya remember I'm in the army. When the colonel calls, I can't say no."

Helga sat up with a big smile on her face. "You remembered. You called me Oraya, that makes my day."

Matt dressed in a hurry, gave Helga a hug and a kiss and hurried over to the colonel's office. Within the small detachment of military advisors, relations were very informal. Without reporting in or saluting Matt sat down. "What's up Fred. Why the hurry?"

"This came in on our unsecured fax." He handed Matt a sheet of paper.

ISIS Attacks Near Irbil, Iraq, Repelled by Peshmerga: Kurds

ISIS launched several waves of attacks in northern Iraq late Tuesday, engaging in close-quarters combat with Kurdish forces before being repelled by reinforcements and airstrikes, officials said.

The jihadis attacked from several directions near the towns of Gewr and Makhmour, southwest of Irbil, according to the Kurdistan Region Security Council (KRSC). They were armed with mortars, rocket-propelled grenades, and heavy machine guns.

The ISIS fighters were driven back by U.S.-led coalition airstrikes, and at least 30 of their number were killed including an emir known as Abu Yaqin who was leading the attacks, the KRSC said in a statement.

By 3 a.m. local time on Wednesday (7 p.m. ET Tuesday), the Kurdish forces were in "complete control and forced ISIS fighters to flee and abandon dead bodies in the battlefield," the statement said.

Earlier, Kurdish and Iraqi officials told NBC News that Kurdish forces had suffered an unspecified number of causalities during the assault.

The KRSC statement added: "Recent gains by [Kurdish] Peshmerga forces in major offensives...have severally disrupted [ISIS's] freedom of movement and its ability send supplies and reinforcements.

After Matt finished reading the article Fred continued. "The fact that ISIS was armed with mortars, rocket-propelled grenades and heavy machine guns worries the Pentagon especially in light of our reports that the Peshmerga has very little in the way of advanced weaponry."

This was good news to Matt. "I'm glad someone over there is finally waking up. There is very little I can do for them without some modern equipment. All they have are some outdated SMAW shoulder launched rockets. They hardly need a US advisor for that."

"Hold on Matt. You're getting your wish. I received a top-secret message from General Bradley in the Pentagon. 'Against the wishes of the Turks, we are going ahead with shipments of weapons to the Kurds. They are getting Javelins, our best shoulder fired missile and the heavier BGM-71 Tow missile system.'"

Matt got excited. "Jesus, who in the hell is going to teach them how to use those babies!"

"You!"

"What do you mean me? All by myself?"

"Not quite. They are sending an entire unit of trained personnel, and since you are already over here, you'll be in charge."

"Why me?"

"Because it's your field of expertise and you spent more than a year in Afghanistan working with exactly the same equipment."

"What about you?"

"Since the type of weapons we will be supplying is top secret, it can't appear that they are sending in a unit of missile and rocket specialists. I, Captain Corso, and the rest of the men and women here are being rotated back to the US and the new people will be listed as replacements."

"I don't have enough rank to be the senior officer in charge."

"They've taken care of that. I didn't want to unceremoniously spring it on you but here is the order promoting you to Lieutenant Colonel."

Matt stared at the order. "My promotion was still two years out."

"Normally yes. But in time of war rank comes quickly. Especially if they need you in a certain position. Congratulations, Colonel!"

"And good things come in two! Helga and I are hitting it off really well."

"I'm aware what is going on Matt, and I have to warn you again; go slow. The lady is a really big deal. And that dam she is in charge of maintaining is the reason the US changed its policy about arming the Kurds. If we lose that dam, we haven't got a prayer of getting Mosul back, let alone driving ISIS out of Kirkuk. Don't forget the strategic position of the oilfields."

"I guess I just have to do a good job protecting her and the dam. Then both the US and I will be happy."

"Rumor has it you had to save each other yesterday during the assault on the dam."

"So you see, we need each other. By the way what are the chances of the new people bringing me a set of brass and some insignia patches for my fatigues? The nearest place I can get that stuff is probably the PX in Baghdad, but I won't get there anytime soon."

"No need. I still have all my Lieutenant Colonel stuff. Including some fancy mortar boards. You're welcome to them."

"That's very kind of you Fred, but I can wait till the new crew gets here."

"No, I insist. It will be my honor to have a recipient of the Distinguished Service Cross wear my insignias."

"How did you know about my medal?"

"It's part of your personnel file. During your first tour in Afghanistan you rescued two pilots from a downed Apache."

"Yeah. Those guys helped protect us while my unit was being rescued from an ambush. They prevented the Taliban from slaughtering us while we tried to climb aboard the rescue helicopters. Unfortunately a Taliban brought them down with a shoulder missile. They were helpless; of course I went to get them."

"From the report in you personnel file it wasn't so simple. The report describes that there was a lot more to it than just going back to get them. I read the whole thing. Besides, one of the pilots you pulled from that burning helicopter is a buddy of mine. He told me that when you saw that the Apache gunship covering your unit's evacuation from the air had been hit by a missile, you jumped out of the last helicopter evacuating your unit. You rescued the crew from the downed aircraft. He claims you pulled him to safety while holding back the advancing Taliban combatants.

"Bullets were whizzing past barely missing the two of you. He was scared stiff, but you were icily calm and said, 'Hand me that M240 you grabbed from the plane so I can keep those fuckers from coming closer.' You dragged my friend to safety while keeping the Taliban fighters pinned down with bursts from the M240 machine gun. When he told you his co-pilot was still stuck in the wreck, you went back to get him. Despite getting hit twice by enemy fire, you managed to free the wounded co-pilot and drag him into the clump of woods where you had left my friend. You held off the Taliban troops until other Apache and Blackhawk helicopters arrived to pick you up. My friend was amazed at your marksmanship. You didn't waste a bullet.

"When you ran out of ammunition, my friend thought he surely was going to die. A Taliban soldier had circled around and attacked the three of you from the rear. You spun around and hit him with the M240. The butt of the M240 just about disintegrated his head. There was a lot of shouting as more Taliban fighters approached from the back. Both pilots were sure they were done for but you grabbed the short barreled .44 Magnum the co-pilot had strapped to his chest and rushed to where the shouting was coming from. The shouting increased followed by a lot of gunfire. The pilots prayed waiting for the Taliban soldiers to emerge from the bushes. Instead you came crawling out, your uniform covered in blood and waiving the empty .44 magnum above your head. My friend swears you were grinning when you said, 'Sweet little gun; those assholes didn't have a chance.' Moments later the sound of approaching helicopters drove the enemy remaining away."

Matt brushed it off. "It wasn't as dramatic as it sounds. Those guys in the Apaches always swooped in to protect us when we got pinned down. It was time to return the favor."

Fred did not agree. "Don't know, but my buddy thinks you should have gotten the Medal of Honor."

Chapter Six

After the colonel left, Matt was assigned to the roomy commander's quarters and Helga moved in with him. It was against army rules, but they did not care. It shortened her commute to the dam considerably, and they got to spend much more time together. Whenever they got a chance to break away, they returned to her apartment in Irbil and worked out in the gym. On one of their trips back to her apartment, Matt asked if Helga missed her daily workout. She replied, "I have a new addiction. This is so much better; I love my new life." They arrived at her apartment and she started heading for the bedroom. "Right now I have something else in mind. My workout can wait. Follow me I need a special warm-up exercise. You've been so busy this last week and I missed our intimate moments. "

Matt did not need much encouragement. *It's not only her incredible body and that beautiful face. I can't help it; I long to be with her.* His brain was still reeling from the surprising developments of the last few days, and he was longing to spend some time in the arms of his lover.

Thinking back on the past week he was still uneasy that he had not gotten any prior notice of the sensitive mission he would be heading. At first, he had not noticed anything unusual when the replacement unit of advisors arrived. But then Tony Caroni came into his office and introduced himself as a DA civilian. "I'm here to further test the successor to the Javelin missile, the Avenger 11.

The Avenger 11 is an updated version of the TOW guided missile, but it's the size of the shoulder fired Javelin."

Matt had to admit that he had never heard of the Avenger 11. Tony went on to explain. "That's because the whole project has been and still is top secret on a need to know basis only. So far, this missile has only been tested on proving grounds in the States, and this is the first time the army has shipped a small unit overseas to test the missile in combat."

"I've worked with the TOW in Afghanistan."

"I assume that's why the army put you in charge of the crew I brought with me. If you liked the accuracy of the TOW, colonel, you'll love this baby. The Avenger system is based on a newly developed chip. We sight in on the target using a regular gun scope. A chip in the missile records an image of the target. Not just the outline but all the details. When we fire the Avenger it seeks out that exact image and destroys it. It can record images from a single individual up to a sixty foot building."

"How many of those Avenger missiles did they ship over here?"

"Sorry, sir. I can't disclose that. We brought about five thousand pounds of military equipment with us. Most of that were Javelin missiles with launch units. A number of Avengers were mixed in. Once the whole lot is fired, we'll report the individual performance of each missile back to the Pentagon. Based on that report the powers that be will decide if the army starts deploying the Avenger 11 on a bigger scale."

"What is my position if I'm not involved in the actual tests?"

"Come on colonel. I'm a civilian contractor. Don't ask me. You get your orders through the chain of command. You're in charge of the unit, and that includes me. You direct our deployment and make sure we're embedded with the most reliable Peshmerga fighters. I hope you're not a stickler for discipline. They sent you a bunch of soldiers, but basically they are nerds selected for their training in electronics and their high security clearance. I have worked side by side with this same group of men; they are the best."

"The two warrant officers are women."

"What's the dif? To me they're all soldiers. I like to tease them and call them lifers."

Making love to Helga made Matt forget his worries about being in charge of this so-called group of nerds and the top secret missiles they would be handling. Helga and he skipped their planned work out and spend the rest of the evening cuddling in Helga's king-sized bed. When he whispered in her ear, "Oraya I love you." Helga responded by snuggling even closer and placing his hand on her breasts.

"Here, play with my nipples. I love to feel you stroke my body. Baby, do you realize how great that is! Just a few weeks ago, I could not imagine a man even touching my body. Then you came into my life and I can't get enough of your touch. Finally, I love my body... don't worry I love yours too." Helga ran her fingers over Matt's scars. "This looks like it was more than just a flesh wound. Honey, I think you were badly wounded."

"I was very lucky they did not hit any vital organs, but I did spend some time in the hospital. Compared to the others on my ward, I could not think of myself as wounded." Matt pulled away and sat up straight. "We have to be realistic and face it; this can't last."

Helga was still holding his hand with which he had been stroking her breast. "What the hell are you talking about?"

"You, me, our relationship will break up eventually."

Helga was close to tears. "You don't really love me after all?"

"No, no that's not it. I'm nuts about you. But you're a beautiful woman with a big-time job, probably earning more than our local generals. As you said - I'm the first guy you're having an intimate relationship with, but I won't be able to hold on to you."

"I can't believe what you're saying. Do you really believe that I could leave you for the very next guy who is nice to me?"

"No, of course not. But you're very attractive and smart, and once you stop pushing men away there will be a lot of them far better than me who will chase after you."

"And what does this *far better than me* mean?"

"Oh, you know, I'm just a lieutenant colonel in the army. There will be guys with big careers who own or manage a large company or are successful in some other field."

Helga let go of Matt's hand and pretended to slap his face. "That's the last time I want to hear such nonsense. That type of hogwash is pretty insulting. No, I will not fall for any old attractive prince charming who might come along. Like it or not, you're my prince and you're stuck with me!" With that Helga pulled Matt close and gave him a long wet kiss. When she came up for air she turned things around. "And why is a hunk like you still available for a gal like me?"

Matt took a while to answer. Finally, he decided to tell Helga the story he had buried for years. "Since you were brutally honest with me and held nothing back about your past I owe you the same."

"Are you bi-sexual or something?"

"No, it's nothing like that. It goes back - all the way back to college. I went to Stanford on a full scholarship and studied engineering. In my junior year I started dating Marybeth McDowell. It got pretty serious between us, and her father did not like it. He managed a hedge fund and was pretty loaded. Marybeth was the apple of his eye. She was spoiled rotten. After the homecoming game that year, we went to several parties, and it got pretty late. Marybeth was driving me home in her fancy sports car, and I repeatedly told her to slow down. She had been drinking at the various parties so I knew she was a little tipsy. I should have stopped her from driving and taken the wheel, but I knew I wasn't completely sober either.

"Where Embarcadero Road becomes Galvez Street she lost control and we crashed. Neither of us was wearing a seatbelt and we were both thrown clear of the car. She died on the way to the hospital. Obviously I survived, but I spent a long time in the hospital. While I was in the hospital Marybeth's father spent a lot of time and effort trying to prove that contrary to the police report, I was driving at the time of the accident. At first he succeeded, and I was kicked out of school and charged with negligent homicide. Through the diligent work of a forensic expert in the police department, I was eventually cleared. I joined the army, and that made it possible for me to finish my schooling and get my engineering degree. The army sent me to OCS, and I was commissioned a second lieutenant. The army rescued me and it became my whole life. As they say, I eat, drink and sleep army. I volunteer for every mission and don't mind getting stationed in an outpost like this. That did not leave any room for a social life."

Helga had been listening carefully. "Both of us had to go through a lot of pain and sorrow in order to meet here in this outpost. For my part, I think it was worth it. I've never been happier in my life. I'm crazy about you and accept what I went through to get this reward."

Matt reached for her and hugged her tightly. "You said what I was thinking!"

Chapter Seven

Matt was on his way to his office in the headquarters building when Chief Warrant Officer Linsey Curry caught up to him. "Colonel Ramsey, I would like to have a word with you."

"Sure, Chief Curry, what's on your mind?"

"Not here, sir. Could we speak in your office, privately?"

"Of course, let's go on in."

Once they were in Matt's office, Linsey said, "This has to remain confidential, sir."

"I understand; sit down and tell me what is going on." Matt sat down behind his desk and motioned for Linsey to take one of the chairs in front of the desk.

"This concerns Toni Caroni."

Matt immediately suspected some kind of harassment.

Linsey had to laugh. "No sir, that's another story. As you know, Toni is one of the developers of the Avenger 11 and is sort of on loan from Aerodynamics, Inc., the manufacturer, to the army while we test its capabilities."

"Yes, he told me."

"The actual testing is done by our crew of army technicians. Chief Williams and I are charged with keeping careful records on the performance of each missile as compared to the older Javelins. Reliability is a vital part of the tests. Toni tries to influence our reports."

"What exactly do you mean by that?"

"Part of each report is objective. It involves a checklist to be filled in with yes or no. The remainder of the report is somewhat subjective, and Toni has repeatedly tried to get us to make our conclusions more favorable."

"Is he supposed to have access to your reports?"

"As far as I know there is no official protocol for that. But Jenny Williams freely shares the reports with him."

"Can't you tell her that it would be better not to let Toni see the reports, especially since he, as the developer, is not a neutral party?"

"There are two problems with that. She's a warrant five and I am a four. And besides the fact that she outranks me, she sleeps with the guy. That's been an open secret since we started testing the Avenger back in the States."

"Why didn't you report that he was interfering with your reporting while you were testing in the States?"

Linsey became frustrated. "I did, sir."

"And?"

"I got nowhere. Jenny convinced everybody that I had a crush on Toni and was jealous of her. If they didn't need me for this project, because of my long career testing Javelin and Tow missiles, I would have gotten in trouble for putting in a false report. It did cost me a promotion in rank. I got passed over while Jenny made Chief Warrant Officer Five."

"Why should I believe you now and not follow the conclusions they made back in the States?"

Linsey's frustration turned to hostility. "I hate that creep! He tried to grope me the very first time we were in the field testing! That was even before he took up with

Jenny. Sir, I did not come to you to tell stories about Jenny, but ever since I have known that dame she has been rolling in the hay with any guy that would have her."

Matt held up his hands in a motion meant to calm down Linsey. "Wow, calm down! I'm not the enemy. I never said I did not believe you. As your commander I am responsible to find out what exactly is going on. Trust me. To start with, I'll give you the benefit of the doubt. Give me some more details."

"Sir, it's my duty to report that several reports have been filed that would indicate that the Avenger rocket is much more reliable than it is."

"If that was your finding, why did you let those reports go through?"

"Jenny Williams outranks me, and she files the final copy of our report. She edits my portion."

"How do you know that?"

"All our reports are top secret, need-to-know only, and are encrypted and sent by Specialist Six Joel Johnson to the Pentagon."

"How do you know that Jenny edits your portion?"

"Joel did not think that what he personally observed during the tests was accurately reported. He has known me for a long time and asked me to show him my original observations. He saw the discrepancy and asked me to contact you."

"Thank you for bringing this to my attention. Please have Specialist Johnson report to me as soon as possible." As Linsey was leaving his office Matt said, "Don't worry, I'll protect you in this matter. Ask Johnson to drop by my office."

Specialist Johnson was able to corroborate everything that Linsey had told Matt but then he added, "Those two cunts have been at it since we got here."

His outburst made Matt furious. Matt jumped all over him. "Hold on mister. I will not tolerate language like that in my unit. If you can't address our female military personnel properly, you don't belong in the army and certainly not in my unit."

Matt's anger surprised Johnson. He knew he wasn't one of Matt's favorites by a long shot, and he was afraid this might cost him his chance for promotion. "Sorry, sir. I apologize; I did not mean to demean the two women, but they fight all the time. I realize my word choice was inappropriate."

Matt decided to let Johnson off the hook. He accepted his apology despite the fact that this man rubbed him the wrong way. He was always complaining about not having enough money and then went out and bought some ridiculous thing he did not need.

After pondering over the problem for a day Matt decided he could solve it locally. He saw no reason to get the Pentagon involved by reporting the relationship between Warrant Officer Jenny Williams and Toni Caroni. That would only cause a needless delay in the testing of the Avenger and introduce personal drama into the public. Besides, Matt thought it would disrupt his mission to support the Kurds, just at a time when they were making huge progress against ISIS. He issued an order that all reports pertaining to all US manufactured missiles would have to be approved by him. He specifically named reports by Chief Warrant Officer Jenny Williams and Chief

Warrant Officer Linsey Curry. These reports had to be submitted to him. After approval, he would give them to Specialist Joel Johnson who would submit them to higher headquarters. He expected an immediate protest from Jenny Williams.

Instead, Toni Caroni showed up. He came barging into Matt's office like a raging bull. "What the hell do you think you're doing? You can't interfere with Chief Williams's reporting."

Matt remained icy calm. "Oh no? And who says so?"

"The reports on the Avenger are need-to-know only, and you are not cleared to see them."

"So now a DA civilian tells a US army commander what he is cleared to see?"

"You're damn right! I told you in the beginning you had no business with those reports."

"Mr. Caroni if you don't sit down and behave yourself, I'll have you removed from this post. I am the commander and responsible for the performance of the unit under my command. For your information, it has been determined that the reports are unsatisfactory."

"By who!" Caroni screamed.

"As you just reminded me, there is such a thing as need-to-know. And you do not need to know who or what agency decided that. All you may know is that I have taken on the responsibility to see to it that the reports meet the required standards. To streamline the procedure the reports will come directly to me. After I approve them they will go to Johnson for transmittal. I will not and cannot prevent you from discussing the results of the test with both warrant officers, but I will not give you access to their reports. That would only delay things, and according to my information, there is no need for that."

Caroni was not ready to give in. "I developed those damn missiles and should see those reports."

"I am quite aware of the fact you developed the missiles. That's why you're here to help with the tests. But McDowell and Curry are quite capable of writing the reports without your help. And from now on, the army will rely on me to see that they follow the prescribed procedures and follow protocol in issuing their conclusions."

"I don't agree."

"Yes, you've made that quite clear. I'm not going to argue with you. My order stands. You are free to contact anyone in the Pentagon who you think can help you gain access to the reports. Any such order would have to come down through the military chain of command and not from the manufacturer."

"Why do you hate me? What have I done to you to make you take this action?"

"Toni what a silly idea. I don't hate you. On the contrary, I think you're a great addition to this dull out-post. Please don't take this personally; all I'm doing is making sure the Pentagon gets satisfactory reports."

"Yeah…but…"

"Come on Toni, from what I have observed those two women are pretty smart. They know what they're doing. That's why they were selected for this mission. I'll keep an eye on things, and we'll keep the Pentagon off our backs. I'd like to make full colonel someday, and I don't need any complaints about a unit under my command."

Chapter Eight

It kept bothering Matt that if he did not report the discrepancies in the earlier reports, the Pentagon might get an inaccurate view of the accuracy of the Avenger 11. His inability to decide what to do depressed him. It did not help his mood that Helga was in Doha, Qatar, consulting on a newly planned oil well. She would not be back for another week, and he was surprised how much he missed her.

The days dragged by, and it seemed forever, but finally Helga called. She was back in her apartment in Irbil and would need a few days to complete her report and file the billing information for the Qatar consult. Matt wanted to race right over to see her, but he had to wait for the Avenger 11 reports and have Specialist Johnson send them to the Pentagon before he could leave.

It was late in the evening by the time Matt arrived at Helga's apartment. They hugged and kissed as if they had not seen each other in years. Matt had never been in Qatar, so Helga told him all about her experiences there and described the landscape. Despite her animated descriptions, especially of the futuristic hotel she had been staying at, it was clear Matt was in a hurry to go to bed and make love.

Helga was already in bed under the sheets by the time Matt came out of the bathroom. He was still wearing his underwear when he approached the bed. Helga laughed at him. "Hey, have you already forgotten that we sleep in the nude?" She reached out and pulled off his undershirt.

"Hurry up! Take off those underpants. I need that gorgeous naked body of yours against me."

Matt responded quickly. He threw his underpants across the room and crawled under the sheets. Helga held out her arms to receive him and he snuggled tightly against her. His hands found her breasts, and as he stroked her nipples, he said, "Talking about a gorgeous naked body, you're pretty amazing yourself Oraya."

"Keep talking honey! I love it when you say things like that." Matt did not keep talking; he was too busy kissing her. Helga's response once again proved that her past demons were gone; she was content with being a female and all the feelings and emotions that came with this new status.

After all the emotions of their reunion calmed down and they were fully spent from their intense love making, it was Matt who could not let go. He kept Helga in a tight embrace and buried his head in her chest. Helga was not used to this. Her lover was the big, strong soldier she clung to for support; her hero who gave her back her self-image. "Honey, what's the matter? Did I do something wrong?"

"No Oraya, no. You could never do anything wrong; I missed you so much. I've been so miserable since you've been gone."

Helga pulled him even closer into her chest. "I missed you too, baby. I could not fall asleep at night. At first, I blamed it on that strange hotel room, but I kept thinking of you. I'm not comfortable when I'm not lying in your arms. I feel so bare and vulnerable when I'm not with you. Being away from you made me realize how deeply in love and dependent I am on you."

Matt told Helga he felt the same way about her. He desperately wanted to share his problem with her, but was afraid he might reveal army secrets by doing so. *I can't tell her about Jenny Williams changing the reports. I would disclose that the top secret Avenger 11 is being tested by the crew under my command.*

Helga sensed there was something more going on. "Okay my love, I love you more than anything else in the world, and I'm sure you love me deeply too, but there has to be more than me being away for a while that has upset you so much. Want to tell me about it?"

Matt made a quick decision. "Two females arguing over the same guy are creating a problem in the unit under my command."

"Come on Matt. As a lieutenant colonel, you should be able to handle that. I don't know if you can do it in the army, but if that happened in a crew of mine I would send all three of them home and let them fight it out in the US."

"It's not that easy to send military advisors home because of that kind of conflict. It's not covered by any regulations. Most regulations are from the time before we had women over here as part of the advisor force."

"Why don't you discuss it with General Edelman? Last time I was in Bagdad I met with him to discuss how far the US would go in protecting my crew at the hydroelectric power plant here at River Zab."

Matt was surprised. "So you know my commander, General Edelman?"

"Sure do. He's a very nice man, and you should talk to him about your problem. He'll help."

"I might do that, but just because he is nice to a beautiful woman does not mean he is as kind to a lieutenant colonel under his command."

"I'm sure you'll solve the problem and be fair to all of them. Sometimes, good people have their emotions go out of control and they can't help themselves. Now relax, your baby is back home, and she needs some more hugging." Having said that Helga wrapped her legs around Matt and moved her lower body back and forth. That worked wonders. Almost instantly, Matt forget his problems; her motion got him aroused and once again he was all hers.

Chapter Nine

Lieutenant General Edelman leaned across his desk; the look in his eyes told Matt that he was not pleased with the reason for Matt's visit. "You mean to tell me that reports on the tests of the Avenger 11 missile are not accurate?"

"Several of the earlier reports may not be accurate, sir. I have no personal knowledge of the tests but as I reported, Chief Warrant Officer Linsey Curry claims that Chief Warrant Officer Jenny Williams edited her report before it was transmitted to the Pentagon."

"And now you have taken it upon yourself to personally check each report to prevent Chief Williams from tempering with it?"

"Yes, sir."

"What gave you the right to check the reports? The results of the tests are classified top secret, need to know only."

"I am aware of that, sir. I was part of a group of military advisors; they were rotated back to the US. I was left here in Iraq, promoted and placed in charge of the replacements. A DA civilian with the group informed me of their mission to test the Avenger 11. As the unit commander, I certainly had the need to know anything that pertained to the mission of the group. When I was made aware that parts of the reports had been tampered with, it was my duty to insure those reports made by the unit under my command were accurate. That gave me the need to know their content."

General Edelman nodded agreement. "And now that you have brought this situation to my attention, what would you like me to do with it?"

"Sir, tests were conducted in the States before this unit was sent over here to conduct tests in a combat zone. We don't know how many of those earlier test reports contained inaccurate information due to the same situation. We cannot risk having the Pentagon draw conclusions based on inaccurate data. I have been able to notify the Pentagon which reports sent in from my unit contained disputed data. I have no information regarding the earlier reports.

"But the situation is more complicated. When Warrant Officer Curry reported that Warrant Officer Williams had changed her reports I thought I had to report Miss Williams' conduct to the proper authority for disciplinary action. But when I confronted Miss Williams with Miss Curry's accusation she told me a different story. According to Miss Williams, Linsey Curry was dating Toni Caroni before he came aboard as a DA civilian to support the unit testing the Avenger 11. Caroni started dating Williams and dumped Curry. That should have made me question the accuracy of Curry's accusation; but specialist Joel Johnson confirmed the fact that Curry's report had been tampered with.

"Rather than conducting a detailed investigation into this matter and taking the risk that the secret nature of the tests might be jeopardized, I have come to you to propose that the tests be called off and the entire unit be called back to the US for further investigation."

"You do realize what you propose is rather drastic? The Department of the Army will be loath to cancel the tests of the Avenger 11. A lot of money has been poured into this project, and a lot of time will be lost."

"I am fully aware of that. But we can't risk having the Avenger 11 evaluation based on false data. Besides, a crime might have been committed by either of the two warrant officers."

"I tend to agree with you. I'll send Major Cooke to the US to brief General Bradley."

"If I may sir, I have one more item to discuss."

"And what is that?"

"I would like to be assigned to the new group of advisors who may be coming in. Then I could remain here in Iraq and complete my tour in Irbil rather than return to the US with the present group of advisors."

"Irbil is not that attractive; you must like working with the Kurds, those feisty Peshmergas."

"I do admire the fearlessness of the Peshmerga fighters, but that is not it. I have met a woman and I would like to stick around to spend time with her."

"May I ask who?"

Matt was happy to tell the general about his relationship with Helga. "Sir you've met her. Helga Kozlov, the engineer at the hydroelectric power plant we help protect."

"Oh yes. I've met Helga. A beautiful woman, you could do worse, but it confuses me that you have a relationship with her."

Matt knew exactly where this was going and cut it off quickly. "She managed to confuse a lot of people. As a single woman working in areas where she is surrounded mostly by men, she hid behind a façade that made it falsely appear she was not interested in men. In the field, she dressed so men would not be interested in her. After we became friends, she dropped the fake façade with me; we have been living together for some time now."

"Well, congratulations. Like I said she's a beautiful woman and she has a good set of brains to boot. I think I can arrange for you to stay in Irbil. The Kurdish commander Agrin Sivan speaks highly of you. That should help."

Rather than return to Irbil the same day, Matt decided to stay in Baghdad overnight and return to Irbil the next morning. During the evening he met a group of helicopter pilots who had been assigned to temporary duty at Irbil International Airport. Billy Daniels, Matt's driver, had made the roughly three hundred and seventy kilometer trip between Baghdad and Irbil several times, and Matt offered to have the pilots follow them. They met early in the morning and the three military sedans headed out of town in the direction Kirkuk. When they approached Kirkuk, they had already covered three quarters of the way, so they decided to go into town for an early lunch.

Matt liked Saj Express because they had the best pizza in Kirkuk. They found parking near the restaurant on the Baghdad road. It was still early for lunch, and the restaurant was not crowded. The staff spoke fluent English, so they had no trouble ordering.

Jonathan, a young first lieutenant asked, "Colonel, should we try one of their local beers?"

Matt was slightly annoyed. The lieutenant should know better. "While we're traveling in uniform we're expected to refrain from consuming alcoholic drinks. You should stick to a coke or something unique like sharbat; it's pretty decent." Matt had hardly finished his sentence when an armed man dressed in camouflage burst through the restaurant door. He sprayed the restaurant with short bursts from his AK 40; the noise was deafening.

"Hit the deck!" Matt yelled. Without thinking, he raced for the armed man. He grabbed the gun and the two of them fell to the ground. A fierce struggle followed. Before anyone could reach them to assist Matt, the gun went off. Blood spattered; Matt rolled over slowly. His uniform was covered with blood, but he was not hurt. By that time two of the pilots had reached him and pulled him up. When they were sure he was okay, they checked the limp body of the assailant. He was dead; the gaping hole in his chest was still bleeding.

"Over here, we need help," one of the pilots was kneeling next to two bodies lying on the ground. Billy Daniels and Jonathan, the young lieutenant, had been hit. Billy was badly wounded, but still conscious; Jonathan had been struck in the head. He was dead.

Matt shouted for one of the pilots to pick up the AK 40 and guard the door in case the assailant had one or more accomplices. He shouted for the restaurant staff to call an ambulance. Next, he called for help on his military phone. "This is Lieutenant Colonel Ramsey. A gunman has assaulted us… location restaurant Saj Express, Baghdad road, Kirkuk."

The person on the other end asked for more details. "Yes, the assailant is neutralized. The wounded soldier will be transported to a local hospital. I'll call in the exact location when I have it; we'll need to airlift him to our nearest army hospital. The body of the deceased will be taken by army sedan back to Baghdad. Please intercept and offer assistance on main highway."

When Matt ended his call he turned to the pilots. "Hurry get Jonathan's body into one of the cars and hightail it back to Baghdad. Get out of Kirkuk as soon as possible; no way of knowing if this is an isolated attack or what else is brewing here in Saddam Hussein's home town."

The pilot who had been tending to Billy's wounds asked what would happen to Billy. Matt assured him that he would stay with him and get him to a US facility as soon as possible.

Moments after the pilots left with Jonathan's body, the Iraq ambulance arrived. The attendants checked Billy's wounds. After they stopped most of the bleeding, they placed him on a gurney and wheeled him out to the ambulance. Billy panicked, "Sir, don't leave me! I don't want to go with them!"

Matt put his hand on Billy's shoulder. "Don't worry. I'm coming along. I'll get you to a US hospital as soon as they stabilize your wounds." When Matt tried to get into the ambulance with Billy the medics stopped him. One of the restaurant staff explained that the ambulance could only take a wounded person to the hospital. Matt pointed to the blood on his shirt and pointed to a spot on his side. "I'm wounded here; I'll need a doctor to look at my wound." This was translated for the medics, and they allowed Matt to get into the ambulance where an anxious Billy grabbed hold of his hand. "Sir, where are they taking me? Are you sure it's okay? They could take us to an Al-Qaida or ISIS camp."

"Trust me, Billy. We're going to have you treated at the local hospital and then our guys will come and get us."

The medic signaled Matt that he was about to give Billy a shot of morphine to kill the pain. Matt explained to Billy that it was okay to have the man give him an injection. It would help stop his pain. On the way to the hospital, the two medics treating Billy managed to further stop the bleeding from his abdomen, but there was not much they could do for his left leg which had been riddled by the bullets sprayed from the AK 40.

On arrival at the hospital, Matt called in their exact location. He had inquired where the helicopter could land and was relieved to be able to report that there was a landing pad on the roof of the hospital. Meanwhile the Iraq doctors did as much as they could to stabilize Billy while waiting for the army medevac helicopter.

The hospital orderlies with a heavily sedated Billy on a gurney had just arrived on the roof of the hospital when Matt heard the distinctive sound of approaching helicopters. Matt looked up and was surprised to see three helicopters overhead. A HH-60 medevac helicopter was escorted by two AH-64 Apache gunships. The medevac helicopter touched down on the helipad while the two gunships circled overhead. Two crewmen jumped out and expertly transferred Billy from the gurney onto a stretcher which they lifted into the helicopter. As the helicopter was lifting off, the crew chief leaned out of the open door and shouted to Matt, "Sir, quick over here, jump aboard. We can't leave you alone here in Kirkuk. We came with an escort because headquarters expects more trouble here from ISIS or maybe from some leftover remnant of Hussein's Republican Guard."

The helicopters headed for the U.S. Military Medical Center in Balad, north of Baghdad. The medevac chopper was given immediate clearance to land on the bustling helicopter pad on the military airbase. Billy was taken into one of the many canvas tents that served as emergency rooms. Moments later, due to the seriousness of his condition, he was taken to a shipping container that had been converted into an operating room. Matt was allowed inside. He spoke to one of the surgeons. "Will he make it doc?"

The doctor was annoyed. "Colonel, please step outside and leave this to us. We are not in the habit of losing soldiers. In the unlikely case we can't handle his injuries here, he'll be put on one of those grey C-17 cargo planes parked out there and flown to Landstuhl, Germany."

Satisfied that Billy was in good hands, Matt started looking for the best way to get back to his unit in the Centri 4 compound near Irbil.

Chapter Ten

Matt was exhausted when he finally got back to Centri 4. When he opened the door to his room, Helga flew into his arms. She was hysterical. "Oh my God…I was so afraid. I thought they might have killed you." She held him so tightly Matt could hardly breathe. "Why didn't you call… I was going out of my mind worrying about you! Commander Sivan told me you had been ambushed in Kirkuk and he didn't know if you had survived. You didn't answer your phone!"

"I did not take my cell phone with me when I went to see General Edelman. It's right here in my dresser drawer. You didn't hear it ring because it's not turned on. I'm so sorry sweetheart, but I couldn't call on my military phone."

Helga was holding on so tightly that Matt almost stumbled when he tried to walk further into the room. Holding on tightly Helga said, "You can't die on me! You can't! You're everything I have; I don't want to live without you. I can't make it without you. I don't want to go back to who I was before I loved you."

Matt managed to disentangle himself from Helga's grip and led her to the bed. When they were both sitting on the bed he said, "Oraya I feel the same way. I don't know what I'd do if something would happen to you. Both of us have chosen to be here in this dangerous place. But some force brought us together in this place, and I'm sure that same force will keep us safe and together."

Helga put her head in his lap. "You think so? You really think we'll be together forever?"

"Yes, my love, it was meant to be that way."

"Hold me a little while longer. I'm still trembling from the thought that I might have lost you. I really meant it when I said I can't go on without you."

Fully dressed the two of them lay hugging and petting until Matt mentioned he had not stopped for dinner. Helga pointed to a big bag of sandwiches next to the closet. "When they knew I was holed up in this room, crying my eyes out because I had not heard from you, one of my staff brought me some food. But I was too upset to eat. I think there is more than enough for two in that bag." Helga got up and unpacked the bag. It contained four Iraqi Chicken Tikka sandwiches, a couple of cokes and a bottle of Iraqi lemonade. The two of them were starved; they quickly devoured the food.

It was late and after Matt had taken a quick shower, they went to bed. They were exhausted from the emotions of the last twenty-four hours. As had become their custom, they were naked. It did not take long before they fell asleep, their naked bodies touching.

In the middle of the night Helga felt Matt stirring. "What's the matter darling, can't you sleep?"

"It's my fault that Billy got injured and that young pilot got killed."

Helga sat up. "What on earth are you talking about?"

"I missed the warning that there was trouble in Kirkuk. We should have driven around the town. I should never have taken them into town."

"That's nonsense! What kind of warning?"

"The crew chief of the medivac chopper told me a warning had been issued that there might be trouble in Kirkuk."

"So what? There is trouble all over this damn country. That's nothing new; they did not tell you not to go into Kirkuk did they?"

"No. But I should have avoided Kirkuk."

"I have received plenty of warnings that ISIS might attack. Should I pull my crew from our position at the dam?"

"Of course not."

"Okay, then stop blaming yourself. Like I said, this whole country is dangerous; you could have been attacked any place. Now stop tossing and turning; I can't sleep without feeling you pressed against me."

Matt lay awake for a long time. The fact that he had missed the warning weighed heavily upon him. Helga turned towards him and in her sleep snuggled against him. The feel of her warm body calmed him down a little, and he finally fell asleep.

The next morning, Matt met with the Kurdish commander Agrin Silvan to coordinate the deployment of his unit in support of the Kurdish advance on Mosul. To Matt's surprise, Commander Silvan had received a full report of the Kirkuk incident. "I hear you are a hero, Colonel Ramsey. Those pilots you saved in Kirkuk reported how your quick response saved them from being mowed down by the assailant. I knew you were a brave man, but that is worthy of praise. The report I got rightly speaks of you as a hero."

"I'm not. I shouldn't have taken those men into Kirkuk."

"What makes you say that?"

"There was a warning that there could be trouble in Kirkuk."

"Yes there was, but at what time were you in Kirkuk?"

"We stopped for lunch around eleven."

"According to my records the warning was issued at eleven forty-six. If I read the report of the incident correctly, at that time you were already in the Iraqi hospital with the wounded soldier. Colonel, that warning was issued based on *your* call for medical assistance."

"Hold on. Are you telling me there was no warning before we stopped for lunch?"

"That's right colonel; the warning was based on your report of the attack. So, you're feeling guilty about stopping in Kirkuk is bullshit."

Matt's feeling of guilt vanished and he was able to laugh at Agrin's very American expression. "Your English is excellent; where did you pick up expressions like bullshit?"

"I was born in New York City, in Queens. My mother came from Puerto Rico, and my father was an immigrant from Iraq. He called the area Kurdistan. When he became tired of driving a cab and saw no chance for promotion, he returned to his family in Kurdistan. I was seven, and against my mother's wishes he took me along. For years she tried to get me back, but the courts in Iraq would not cooperate."

"Did you ever go back to see your mother?"

"Nah, she died of an overdose before I would have been old enough to do that. She was an addict; that was the main reason she never got custody of me."

"If you were born in the States, you're an American!"

"No way! I like you guys a lot, but I'm a proud Kurd. I grew up among my Kurdish family; my grandmother has been my mom since I was seven. We moved to Irbil when I was fourteen."

"Wow! Who knew? That's some story. No wonder you understand the relationship between the Peshmerga and us, the US advisors, so well."

"Speaking of understanding relationships, colonel, I hope I'm not too presumptuous when I mention that I observed some friction between the two women in your unit. I believe it has something to do with Toni Caroni the civilian."

"Yes, I'm aware of that. The two don't get along."

"This Caroni fellow does not help the situation. And, if I may be so bold to say, having a lady stay in your room here on post does not set a good example."

Matt's first reaction was to get mad and tell Agrin that his relationship with Helga was none of his business. But before he could respond, Agrin continued.

"Miss Kozlov, she wants me to call her Helga, is an exceptional woman. I have the greatest respect for both of you, and I am not faulting you two. With the dangerous conditions of the last month, she should not be traveling alone at night back to Irbil. You are right to keep her here on the base, and judging from her reaction when I told her about the ambush, I understand why she is staying with you in your room. I understand all of it. She's beautiful, but it still sets a bad example when the commander has a woman staying in his room on a tactical base."

The man was right, and Matt knew it. "The only thing I can say is that I hope the rest of my behavior makes up for this less than perfect example."

"That it does! Working with you has been great. In the past I've had to work with groups of advisors who acted more like strict school teachers than advisors. Sort of 'I'm the boss and you must do as I say.' You're different, and you teach your men to be different."

"Nice of you to say."

"The US Army must think pretty highly of you. In the past we had here at Centri 4 a group of advisors led by a full colonel, you, and several ranking sergeants. When that group went back to the States, they left you by yourself in charge of the new group of advisors. That shows me they have great confidence in your leadership. While I'm freely making comments, I have one more piece of advice. Actually, it's an urgent request. Please stop traveling around Iraq in an US Army sedan driven by a US soldier. It's not safe! Ammar, your Iraq translator, is an excellent driver. Let him drive you around in that old half ton truck of his. He'll keep you safe; he knows the ins and outs of this country better than anyone I know. Things are heating up, I expect the assault to take back Mosul to start any time now, and ISIS is moving extra fighters into the area."

Chapter Eleven

Matt informed the personnel conducting the test of the Avenger 11 missile that the Pentagon had shortened the test period and they would be returning to the US. A few days later, instructions arrived to securely pack the remaining Avenger 11 missiles and send them back to Aerodynamics, Inc. labeling the shipment defective Javelin missiles returned for inspection.

Matt expected to hear a lot of protest from Toni Caroni. Surprisingly, Toni did not even question why the test period was shortened. The only complaint came from Specialist Joel Johnson. Besides objecting to all the paperwork he had to prepare for Matt's signature, he moaned about missing the combat pay which he could have collected while serving in Iraq. This was not surprising. Johnson was always bugging Matt to recommend him for promotion so he could earn more. The relocation orders for the advisors came through in the same month that the Iraq government launched the assault to retake Mosul. As part of the push, two hundred US Marines and four 155-millimeter howitzer cannons were sent to Firebase Bell, an outpost near Makhmour where US advisors had trained Iraqi troops for the assault on Mosul. As the Iraq Rapid Response Force advanced, ISIS was forced out of Ramadi, west of Baghdad, Hit, and parts of Sinjar in northern Iraq.

Al Jazeera's Mohammed Adow reported from Gwer, in northern Iraq:

Iraqi army readies for assault on Mosul
Senior government officials visit Erbil to win support of Kurdish Peshmerga forces for planned offensive against ISIL

Commander Agrin Sivan and his Peshmerga fighters were deployed in an attempt to contain the city from the north and keep it isolated from additional Islamic State fighters to the west. The Iraq Rapid Response Force was the primary attack force during the assault. As the lone US military advisor left in Centri 4, Matt was embedded with the Kurds.

When she was told that Matt would be heading towards Mosul with the Kurds, Helga was devastated. "Matt don't go, please. It's suicide storming that city. The number of casualties will be unbelievable."

"I won't be up front. I'll be calling in artillery strikes from a distance."

"Matt you know that isn't true; you'll be up at the front among the troops."

"Agrin and his troops know what they're doing. They are the most experienced fighters in Iraq. They won't get us killed." Helga was not convinced.

To protect the hydroelectric dam Agrin left behind a small group of his fighters. Ronahi Judi was in charge of that group and Agrin made her responsible for Helga's safety. Ronahi insisted that Helga, during Matt's absence, not move back to her apartment in Irbil. She wanted Helga within the safety of Centri 4.

The night before Matt moved out with the Peshmerga, Helga was inconsolable. They always slept in each other's arms, but this time she held on to Matt as if she was trying to prevent him from leaving. She could not stop crying. After Matt left, Helga devoured every newspaper she could get her hands on. The official government reports were optimistic, but Ronahi told her a different story. She reported that in a bitter battle ISIS had repelled the Iraqi assault. She claimed that the Peshmerga fighters were bogged down due to a lack of ammunition and supplies. Helga was aware that Matt and the US advisors were only unofficially supporting the Kurds, but she could not understand why the US would not help with arms and supplies. But. Finally. It did happen; the newspapers carried it on the front page:

US officials sign deal to give Peshmerga units some $415m for ammunition, food, pay, and medical equipment.

When the story broke the celebrations in Irbil went on long into the night. The excitement continued several weeks later when the headlines read:

Kurdish Peshmerga forces claim to be in control of nearly three-quarters of Bashiqa, a town 13km east of Mosul city.

Ronahi followed the battle blow by blow and kept Helga informed. She gave a vivid account of how government troops backed by jets and gunships retook the airport which gave them access to Mosul from the south. Next, followed the push into the southwest of Mosul. Fearful that Helga could not handle it, Ronahi did not tell her that Agrin's Peshmerga unit headed the assault on the southwest of the city and was engaged in close combat with the ISIS rebels.

Agrin and his men had advanced into Al-Maamun a small neighborhood on the outer edge of the city when ISIS launched a fierce counter attack. They surrounded Agrin's fighters and cut them off from the rest of the Peshmerga. There was a report that Agrin might be wounded.

Chapter Twelve

Matt was at the airport assisting an artillery unit firing at ISIS positions inside Mosul. When ISIS broke through and surrounded Agrin and his men, they had to cease firing because of the possibility of hitting the Kurds.

Matt received the message that Agrin had been wounded. He went to find Colonel Al-Rubaye who commanded the Iraqi Rapid Response force during the assault. "Colonel, are you sending troops to support Commander Sivan?"

"Starting tomorrow we have planned a major assault on the center of the city. I do not have enough trained officers to launch a separate attack. I hope they can hold out till we can get to them."

"Colonel you know darn well that they don't have a chance to survive the night. They need help now!"

"I'm sorry, I can't help. This is not like your American army; I only have a few trained officers to lead my men."

Matt did not stop to argue. He went directly to the area where the Marines were. He found Captain Jenkins who was with the group supporting the Iraqis with heavy howitzer cannons. He had served with Tom Jenkins in Afghanistan. "Tom, a unit of the Peshmerga in which I'm embedded is surrounded in Al-Maamun on the edge of the city. I need your help to get them out."

"Just the two of us?"

Mattt laughed at the response. "That sounds like the feisty young Tom I knew in Afghanistan. No, buddy, I'm not that crazy; I'll get some men from Colonel Al-Rubaye."

Tom Jenkins agreed to help. Matt returned to ask Colonel Al-Rubaye for a dozen men. The colonel was not pleased, but Matt pushed hard and got the men.

Darkness was setting in when two groups headed for Al-Maamun. One led by Matt and the other by Tom Jenkins. Matt's group approached from the west and Tom's from the east. To distract the ISIS fighters, Tom had arranged a heavy bombardment in the center of the city from the howitzers. Unnoticed, Matt's group reached the houses on the outskirts of town. He instructed his men on how to cover each other while they searched the first house for any traces of ISIS fighters. When they were sure the house was abandoned they settled in and waited for a signal from Tom.

When Tom's group reached the first houses on the east side of town they started firing with machine guns and throwing claymore mines. The ISIS fighter who had surrounded the Kurds rushed to repulse the assault. That was the signal Matt was waiting for, and he and his men moved in to attack the ISIS fighters from the rear. As they stormed in, the embattled Peshmerga soldiers joined them. A fierce gunfight followed; the ISIS fighters did not have a chance. Within ten minutes most of them were dead or had fled.

Matt went to look for Agrin. He did not see him anywhere; he asked one of the Peshmerga soldiers were their commander was. "He stayed behind to cover our retreat when the ISIS fighters overran our position. I saw him run into a three story building. He broke a third story window and used a machine gun to pin down the on storming ISIS soldiers so we could retreat behind a new defense line."

Matt started off in the direction from where Agrin's men had retreated. Most of the ISIS fighters had rushed to the section where Tom and his men were. Matt's group with help of the Agrin's Peshmergas had taken care of those still in the area. Matt spotted two large three story buildings. Assuming there were no longer any ISIS soldiers around he ran into the nearest of the two buildings. He raced up the stairs but made a dead stop halfway up. Bullets were flying passed his head. They were coming from the top of the stairs. Matt dove down the stairs head first and took cover. He had to get up the stairs to find Agrin but first he had to get past the shooter ensconced at the top of the stairs. He could not crawl out of his covered position to attack the gunman. He'd be dead before he got halfway up the stairs. He had no idea if Agrin was being held up there or not, and if he would be in harm's way if he used a grenade; he had no choice.

Matt removed one of the hand grenades he had on his belt and got up on his knees. He took a deep breath and pulled the pin; counted one..two and ran for the stairs. While moving at full speed he heaved the grenade up the stairs and dropped to the floor covering his head with both arms.

When the smoke cleared Matt surveyed the damage. Part of the top of the stairs was gone exposing a big part of the second floor. Part way down the stairs between a heap of rubble Matt saw the mutilated body of an ISIS fighter. Pushing some broken concrete aside Matt managed to reach the second floor. The floor was empty and he rushed to the third floor. Also empty!

Matt hurried on to the next building. This time he carefully checked before going up the stairs. On the third floor he found Agrin badly wounded in front of a window, one hand stretched over his machinegun. He was half conscious but did recognize Matt. "What are you doing here?"

"Thought you might need a ride home."

Agrin did not catch the humor. "Go before they return. I'm dying; they won't take me alive."

"Damn it you're not dying. I'm taking you out of here."

"I can't move. It hurts so bad. Just leave me and go."

From the emergency kit he had taken with him, Matt took out a syringe and gave the half conscious Agrin a heavy dose of morphine.

After consulting with Tom on the best way to bring Agrin back to the airport, Matt went to look for a door. When he found a suitable door he had several men carefully lift Agrin onto that door. Next he placed three men on each side and two men on each end. When they raised the plank the two men in front turned around and grabbed the door behind their back. Carefully, step by step they carried Agrin down the stairs. When they reached the street the rest of the soldiers surrounded them and they started the long track back to the airport. At the outskirts of town Tom and his group of soldiers joined them.

When they reached the airport, Matt tried to arrange to have Agrin airlifted to the hospital in Irbil. He could not locate any available Iraqi helicopters, and he asked the US marines for help. His request was denied because the wounded soldier was not American and US helicopters would not get permission to land at a local Iraqi hospital.

Determined to get the badly wounded Agrin to a hospital as soon as possible, Matt appealed directly to a friend serving with the US Central Command in Iraq. Not to get involved in administrate matters, he made a short unauthorized call to his friend on his personal cell phone which he had accidently taken along. After identifying himself he said, "Donny I need your help. Can you arrange the medical evacuation of an American wounded during the assault on Mosul? We brought him to Mosul airport, he's in critical condition."

The answer was better than he hoped for. "Can you stabilize the patient?"

"Negative. I was only able to give morphine for pain."

"Helicopter on the way. They'll contact Mosul airport for landing instructions have patient ready at landing site."

After he hung up Matt had Ammar in his half ton truck drive him over to the air traffic control tower. The Iraqi air traffic controller on duty directed Matt to the US liaison officer sitting at a nearby desk. Matt explained the situation and got instructions where to wait with Agrin until the helicopter arrived. Next, Matt hurried back to where Ammar was waiting in his truck and they drove to where the Marine unit was stationed.

While waiting for Matt, Tom had the US Marine Medics transfer Agrin to a stretcher and cover his open wounds with sterile bandages to prevent infection. They loaded Agrin onto Ammar's truck and Matt directed them to the helipad where the medical evacuation helicopter was expected to arrive shortly.

Chapter Thirteen

Helga was waiting for Ronahi to bring her the latest news on the assault. When she did not show up, Helga went to look for her. She was surprised to find Ronani in her room, sitting bent over on her bed. Helga was shocked to see that this courageous Peshmerga fighter had been crying.

"Ronahi what happened? Why are you crying?"

"Agrin is badly wounded! They found him and brought him back to the airport. They think he's dying."

"Who's they?"

"Our Kurdish soldiers who were rescued after ISIS surrounded them. I think Matt was with them."

"Matt was in the front lines? I thought he was back at the airport coordinating artillery fire."

"Maybe. Maybe he was there when they brought Agrin in. Can you reach Matt to ask about Agrin.?"

"Probably not, but I'll try. He never takes his personal cell phone into a combat area, but it's worth a try." Helga dialed Matt's phone not expecting him to answer. If he had accidently taken it with him he certainly would not have it turned on.

On the second ring, she heard, "Hello Donny. Is the chopper delayed?"

"Matt darling it's me Helga. Are you okay?"

"Yes, I'm fine but you shouldn't have called on this phone. It's not safe; the bad guys could locate me."

"I'm sorry I know but we have to know how Agrin is. Ronahi is with me."

"Put her on."

"Matt it's me Ronahi, is Agrin with you?"

"Yes he is. He is badly wounded, but we'll get him to the very best doctors. We'll do everything possible to save him."

Matt could hear that Ronahi was crying. "Ronahi do you trust me?"

"Of course"

"Then trust me to do everything possible. For safety I must hang up, private calls are not authorized. Give my love to Helga." The phone went dead.

Helga went over and sat on the bed next to Ronahi. As she wiped Ronahi's tears away she was dying to ask why this beautiful young woman was wearing lipstick and makeup. She looked more like a Hollywood starlet than a soldier. Helga had been surprised to see that many of the female Kurd soldiers wore makeup. Before she came to Iraq, Helga believed that all the Kurdish women had to wear the traditional head scarf. Afraid to insult them she had been hesitant to ask about the makeup. But now sitting with her arm around Ronahi and wiping way her tears she asked.

The question made Ronahi smile. "We want to look beautiful in case we are killed. We have found a great weapon against the murderous fanatics of ISIS. That terror group that sees us women as objects to be enslaved, raped and terrorized hates us. And our weapon against them is makeup."

That broke the tension of the moment and Helga laughed. "Really?"

"Yes. I always do my eyebrows and apply lipstick and mascara before I put on my uniform and make sure my assault rifle functions. Here look." Ronahi removed one of her boots and showed Helga her painted nails. "Look I even paint my toenails."

Helga leaned back still laughing and showed her unpolished toenails. "Guess I don't prepare for battle correctly."

Helga felt she was getting to know Ronahi as a person rather than the tough soldier assigned to guard her. She asked a more personal question. "It's clear you really have strong feelings for Agrin, how long have you known him?"

"I first met him when I was part of the Women Peshmerga of the 2nd Battalion in Sulaymaniyah here in Iraq. He was a dashing young soldier, assigned to our British trainers. I couldn't keep my eyes off him. He never even noticed me. He was all business, everything by the rules. Totally devoted to his duty as a Kurdish officer. I made rank quickly, and at one point was in a position to choose my next assignment. When I heard he was the commander of the Kurdish forces here in Irbil I moved heaven and earth to be stationed under his command here in Centri 4.

"I know he likes me. He has repeatedly recommended me for promotion. He trusts me, but unfortunately he only sees me as a soldier not as a woman."

Chapter Fourteen

A fresh Peshmerga regiment replaced what was left of Agrin's unit on the front lines in Mosul. The heavily decimated contingent returned to Centri 4. Matt did not join the new regiment in Mosul; he was ordered to stay in Centri 4 and wait for new orders. The new order lacked any detail about a new assignment.

The curt message only read, "Report immediately to General Edelman in Baghdad."

To Matt this could only mean two things. Either General Edelman was unable to arrange for him to stay in Iraq, or he was in trouble for having Agrin hospitalized as a US citizen and not disclosing that the wounded soldier was a Peshmerga fighter.

Assuming that it would only be a one day trip, Matt asked Ammar to drive him back and forth to Baghdad. Upon arriving at General Edelman's office Matt was met outside the building by two MPs who asked him to take off his side firearm and give his pistol to them.

Matt had no idea what that was all about; he assumed this was a new security protocol institute after numerous attacks on the headquarters building. The MPs escorted him to General Edelman's office.

The general was sitting behind his desk flanked by his chief of staff and a MP colonel. The general did not bother to return Matt's salute and Matt was shocked by what he said. "Lieutenant Colonel Matthaeus Ramsey, I'm placing you under arrest."

Matt gasped. "For not disclosing that the wounded soldier was Commander Agrin Sivan, the Peshmerga commander?"

General Edelman looked puzzled but quickly regained his composure. "I have no idea what you're talking about. You are under arrest for delivering top secret documents to the Russians."

Matt's chest was pounding, this could not be happening. "Sir you have known me for a long time. You know my service record; you must know that it is impossible for me to have done anything like that."

The general's tones soften a little, "Colonel, I'm not the one accusing you. Military Intelligence claims to have evidence you gave top secret documents to a Russian operative. I've been instructed to place you under arrest and have these two MPs escort you back to Fort Bragg, North Carolina, for trial."

Matt did not even get a chance to notify Helga of his arrest. From the general's office he was taken directly to the airport and put on a plane. Handcuffed and seated between the two MPs, he was flown non-stop to Fort Bragg, North Carolina.

He was held incommunicado for three days in what could be described as half way between a prison cell and a sparsely furnished BOQ room.

On the fourth day two JAG officers came to see him. Colonel Buckley introduced himself and informed Matt that he had been assigned to defend him and that Captain Pentowski would also be part of the defense team. Army Investigator Lt. Colonel Harrison would conduct the preliminary investigation.

Colonel Buckley briefed Matt on the evidence Military Intelligence claimed to have against him. "Several of our intelligence agencies intercepted Russian messages warning their allies that we have a new shoulder fired missile. Copies of tests reports in their possession show that this new missile is being tested against the Javelin. From these reports, they have concluded that this is an updated version of our Tow Guided Missile, but that it is about the same size of the Javelin."

It dawned on Matt that those reports were the top secret documents he was being accused of passing to the Russians. "They think I gave those reports to the Russians?"

"Yes they do."

"Are they nuts? Where the hell do they come off accusing me!"

"Unfortunately, they claim to have a lot of evidence."

"You got to be kidding. A lot of evidence, like what?"

"Calm down, I'll explain. You were not aware of it, but Military Intelligence had you under surveillance."

"This is getting more ridiculous by the minute. If that guy from MI working out of Bagdad was the one keeping me under surveillance it's no wonder the army got a false report on me. That man is a creep. Whenever he questioned someone in my unit he always started by asking about their sex life. The guy is a pervert. On several occasions I had to ask him to leave and stop harassing my troops."

"Calling him names does not help your case. He's not under indictment. You are."

"Why were they spying on me?"

"You're angry, and I understand that. But let me explain. They were not spying; it was a routine investigation. You were having an affair with a Russian national and that calls automatically for an investigation."

"Are you kidding me! Has 1984 come true; big brother is watching me? They think Helga is a spy? Has the whole world gone crazy?"

"Colonel please calm down. I've read the whole dossier prepared by MI to support the charges against you and I want to discuss it with you. Remember, I am on your side. We need to prepare your defense."

Matt was still agitated but he was willing to listen to what Colonel Buckley had to say.

"I agree that it is unusual for MI to monitor your activities just because you were having an affair, but in your case they found it suspicious. Helga Kozlov, the woman you were seeing, is well known by the US Army for the work her company IEDC does for the US and other governments. In army circles she is considered to probably be a lesbian because of the aggressive way she avoids social contact with males. This suddenly changed after she met you. Adding to MI's suspicion was your outspoken support of the Kurds at a time when US troops imbedded in a Peshmerga unit was secret and highly controversial."

Matt wanted to interrupt but Colonel Buckley waved him off.

"Hold on, let me continue, so you know the full story before you reply. It is known that you disobeyed orders and actively engaged in combat on behalf of the Kurds when you led an Iraqi unit into Mosul to free some embattled Peshmerga fighters. This was further aggravated by you when you called for a US military helicopter to evacuate a wounded Peshmerga officer to a US Army hospital."

Again Matt wanted to interrupt. He tried to defend his actions.

Now it was Colonel Buckley who was getting irritated. "Colonel, just let me finish before you respond! You were already under surveillance when a Russian message about our new missile was intercepted. Knowledge of the test results of the Avenger 11 missile by your unit was on a need to know basis. All personnel familiar with the tests results were immediately questioned. During their investigation MI learned that even though you were not granted access to the test reports, you took it upon yourself to authorize yourself to read them and process them.

"Colonel, if I may say so, we have a problem here. They have cited two Court Martial offenses you committed at a time when you were already under surveillance for your close association with Miss Kozlov and your outspoken support of the Kurds to the detriment of the Iraqi government."

It took a while for Matt to digest what Colonel Buckley said. "Wow, they're really after me. What do you think colonel; do you think I handed those reports to the Russians?"

"I'm appointed to defend you, not to judge you. If you plead not guilty I'll do my utmost to help prove your innocence. And if you chose to plead guilty to the charges, I'll fight like hell to get a lenient sentence for you."

"There is no way I can plead guilty to something I did not do. Look at my army record. There is nothing there that shows any sympathy for the Russians or any nation hostile to the US. Everything they dug up can easily be explained."

"Before we get into that I'll ask Captain Pentowski to join us and brief you on the events of the last couple of days."

Captain Pentowski entered the room with an arm full of folders carefully separated by colored stickers indicating their content. After he introduced himself, he briefed Matt on the latest developments.

"At the time of your arrest in Bagdad the US Government formally requested the Iraqi Government for the extradition of Helga Kozlov. But when she heard of your arrest and the charges against you she voluntary returned to the US. On her arrival, she was arrested and charged with spying for Russia. After her arraignment, her employer IEDC posted a ten million dollar bail bond which allowed her to stay in her apartment under house arrest. All her travel documents were confiscated and she is required to wear an electronic bracelet. IEDC responded to her arrest by cancelling all their contracts with the US Government and immediately withdrawing all personnel from US basis."

Matt could not believe what he heard. "Have they gone completely mad? They have nothing to go on. Just because she was born in Russia does not make her a spy. This is crazy. Can I call her?"

"Sorry, no. You're being held incommunicado. That means you can only talk to us and an army investigator if we are present. But I have a folder here which contains a signed offer from the prosecution."

"What the hell is that about?"

"I'll skip the legal language but what it comes down to is that you are offered a reduced sentence if you'll testify against Helga Kozlov."

Matt exploded.

He grabbed the folder out of Captain Pentowski's hands and tried to rip it in half. "They can take this offer and stick it up their ass! Helga is no more guilty than I am. This whole thing is a bunch of horse shit. I'm being set up and I don't know why. I want a lawyer; this whole thing is crazy."

Pentowski looked at Bradley and the latter responded.

"You are free to request other counsel and of course you can hire a civilian lawyer. But I assure you Captain Pentowski and I will be on your side all the way and we'll fight the charges. I promise we'll leave no stone unturned."

"What about Helga?"

"Her case will be handled in federal court, she's a civilian. I wouldn't worry about her. IEDC's corporate lawyer has arranged for her defense. Her lawyers must be pretty good. They kept her out of jail pending trail. That's unusual in spy cases. They must be pretty sure that you'll be acquitted because they have already petitioned the court to postpone her trial until after yours is over."

Hearing that Helga was in good hands calmed Matt down. He knew IEDC was a huge company; having them on their side made him feel less powerless.

Helga and he were not alone in this; they had a powerful ally in fighting this nightmare.

Chapter Fifteen

To prepare for Matt's trail Colonel Buckley and Captain Pentowski requested a list of all the witnesses the prosecution intended to call. There were no surprises. Matt's court marshal started with the presiding officer reading the charges. After Matt pleaded not guilty, Colonel Hickey called the first witness for the prosecution.

MI was allowed to submit their full report. On cross examination, Colonel Buckley made each agent involved in preparing the dossier admit that they had no personal knowledge of Matt contacting any person or agency that might have any connection to Russia. In his rebuttal, Colonel Hickey emphasized that Helga Kozlov, Mattt's reputed lover, was a Russian national.

Next General Edelman was called and asked how Helga was perceived by the army and whether it surprised him that she would have an affair with Matt. He admitted that it did surprise him. He described Helga as a very attractive woman who before she became involved with Lieutenant Colonel Ramsey had stayed away from personal relationships with men.

When Colonel Hickey asked him to explain further; General Edelman said he had presumed Helga was a lesbian. But on cross examination, he added that it was not a bad idea for Helga, since she was mostly stationed in a military environment among men, to stay away from any personal relationship with them.

Colonel Hickey objected when General Edelman was asked if he thought Matt would have any reason to pass secrets to the Russians. The court sustained the objection on grounds that General Edelman's opinion in the matter was not relevant to the case.

As expected, the next group of witnesses for the prosecution could do no more than corroborate the circumstantial evidence against Matt. Jenny Williams expressed doubt as to why it was necessary for Matt to review her report before submitting it together with Linsey's. Linsey Curry on the other hand was glad that her report did not get edited by Jenny.

Toni Caroni testified that he told Matt the reports were need-to-know only, and there was no reason for Matt to check them.

When pressed on cross examination, he did admit that at the time he saw no reason why Matt wanted to review the reports other than Matt's distrust of Jenny Williams.

Specialist Joel Johnson's testimony was a little more damaging. He explained that when both reports were handed to Matt there was ample time to copy them before Matt gave them to him to be transmitted.

Captain Pentowski pressed him hard on this matter, and Johnson had to admit he had never seen Matt take the reports to his office.

Captain Pentowski asked whether there was a copy machine in Matt's office. Johnson said there wasn't. When asked where there was a copy machine, Johnson stated the only one was located in his office. Pentowski pressed further and asked if Matt had been in Johnson's office without Johnson being present. Johnson was evasive, but finally confirmed that Matt could not enter his office while he was not there. Because of all the sensitive equipment he had to follow army regulations and keep his office locked when he was not there.

Captain Pentowski caught Johnson off guard when he asked him if anyone had made extra copies of the reports. "Mr. Johnson you told this court that when both reports were handed to Colonel Ramsey there was ample time to copy them before he gave them to you to be transmitted. Is it possible those reports were copied *before* they were given to the colonel?"

Johnson seemed flustered. "I can't say for sure but I don't think that would have been possible." Captain Pentowski tried to push the issue but was stopped when the prosecution claimed he was badgering the witness and the court agreed.

To show there was nothing in Matt's background to support any suspicion about his loyalty to the United States, the defense introduced several character witnesses.

Each witness testified that they knew Matt as a dedicated officer who through his service showed his dedication and a great love of his country.

The court did not allow any testimony regarding the character of Helga Kozlov. The defense had argued that her character was pivotal to Matt's defense and that without her there were no grounds for the case against him. The defense had called several executives of IEDC to testify, but the court held that they did not know enough about her background to be able to testify as to her character.

The government also prevented the Kurdish commander Agrin Sivan from entering the country in order to testify on Matt's behalf. The defense argued that this was detrimental to their case because Agrin would have testified that Matt supported the Peshmerga forces on behalf of the Iraqi war effort and that would have argued against him helping the Russians.

The final dispute between Colonel Hickey and the defense came when Colonel Hickey introduced that Matt had been expelled from Stanford because he was charged with negligent homicide. This brought Colonel Buckley to his feet. He demanded that Colonel Hickey correct the record by showing that Matt had been cleared of all wrong doing. The court would not go so far in making Colonel Hickey state for the record that Matt had been cleared.

There was no evidence a court had cleared him. Colonel Buckley was on his feet and demanded time to produce police records dated back to the time of the accident. The court refused, and Colonel Buckley demanded a mistrial. This too was refused, and the court retired to discuss the case.

The very next day the court announced its finding. The defense team was stunned; the verdict was guilty. The sentence that followed was a dishonorable discharge and confinement for twenty-five years.

Colonel Buckley rushed to explain to Matt that every general court marshal conviction is reviewed automatically by the convening authority. The convening authority can reduce the sentence and or discharge, but they cannot increase it. Because of the severity of the charge, his case would automatically be reviewed by the Army Court of Criminal Appeals.

If he was still dissatisfied with the review conducted by the Army Court of Criminal Appeals, he would have the option to appeal to the U.S. Court of Appeals for the Armed Forces.

Chapter Sixteen

During the appeal process, Matt was confined to the same cell he had been held in during the court marshal. He could not have any visitors or make calls to the outside world. He was able to request books and sports magazines. But for the most part, he was bored and worried about his appeal. To his surprise one day a well-dressed man entered his cell. The man introduced himself as James McDowell. "You know me as Jimmy."

Matt thought for a while and asked, "Are you Jimmy McDowell, Marybeth's older brother?"

"Yes, I am."

Matt's kneejerk reaction was to throw the man out. Marybeth's older brother! The guy who had, together with his father, tried everything, including lying, to pin the car accident on him. "Get the hell out of here. You must be delighted to see me in jail, but no matter what you think I was not driving her car that night."

Jimmy expected Matt's hostile reaction. "I'm not gloating, and you've every right to hate me. But before you throw me out, can we talk?"

"How did you get in here anyway?"

"I'm a lawyer, and Colonel Buckley cleared me."

"No way, you're not *my* lawyer!"

"Please can we talk?"

"We have nothing to discuss. You and your father did your best to screw me."

"Yes we did. What we did was terrible, and I have come to tell you I know that."

That caught Matt's attention but before he could say anything Jimmy continued. "My sister played all of us. You, me, and most of all, her father. She charmed us into believing she was a loving daughter and sister and that she loved you. It was tough to find out she was a knifing little bitch. We did not find out until a local drug dealer was arrested and revealed that she was one of his major clients. We knew she spent my father's money freely, but he had no idea she spent so much of it on drugs. When she ran short, she would sell drugs for the dealer to pay off her debt to him. She took full advantage of your popularity on campus by having you take her to every party where she could peddle her drugs behind your back. Finding out who the apple of his eye really was killed my old man. It left me with a guilt complex for what I did to you, which I've never been able to shake."

Matt dropped his hostility towards Jimmy. "Marybeth on drugs. Seems hard to believe, but I have no reason to doubt what you're telling me. Her death hit me harder than being accused of driving the car and causing her death. I knew the latter was not true and that the truth would eventually come out. I loved her, and I wasn't even allowed to mourn her death because of the police investigation."

"Yes, we never considered your feelings. Is it true the two of you were secretly engaged?"

"Yes."

"I've not only come to apologize and tell you how deeply sorry I am. I want to help you prove your innocence. I can't for a moment believe you are guilty of espionage."

"And how would you do that?"

"As I said I'm a lawyer. I'm the senior partner in my firm, McDowell, Gaggiotti and Mukillo. The firm has over nine hundred lawyers spread over six countries. We have connections in many places which include the US Army, the State Department, and even the C.I.A. I'm sure we can help you, and I've already spoken to Colonel Buckley. He said I have to discuss it with you, but he would be delighted to work with me."

PART TWO

Jimmy

Chapter One

After getting Matt's permission, Jimmy McDowell discussed the case with Colonel Buckley and Captain Pentowski. Based on the information he received from them, he instructed several investigators working for his firm to, "Follow the money."

"I want you to dig into the personal life of each person who had any involvement with the test reports that were passed on to the Russians. Analyze their recent purchases and other expenditures to determine if there is any change in their financial position. Don't skip anything. I want to know about every detail no matter how minor."

The first reports he received where on Chief Warrant Officer Linsey Curry. She was cleared from any allegations that she might have falsely accused Jenny Williams of editing her reports. As a result, she was promoted to Chief Warrant Officer Five. Her only income was her army pay and much of it went to support her retired parents living in Arizona.

While clearing Linsey Curry of any wrongdoing, it was determined that Jenny Williams submitted reports that showed the Avenger 11 was more accurate than the tests indicated. A trial would reveal too much detail about the tests, and she was allowed to resign from the service. Two month later she married Toni Caroni.

Jimmy decided to interview the couple himself. Matt had told him about Toni's furious reaction when he was told Matt would collect the reports from Linsey and Jenny and that he would pass them on for transmission to the Pentagon.

Jimmy introduced himself as Matt's civilian defense council. To his surprise Toni was happy to talk to him and immediately inquired about Jimmy's experience. "Have you done any defense work before?"

"Yes, that's my main line of work. I was the lead council on the Victor Morelli case."

Toni was impressed. "Heard of that case. That was a biggie. Glad Colonel Matt is getting a decent defense."

"Don't you think his appointed defense - the two JAG officers - are qualified?"

"That's not it. But from the way the army interviewed me, I have the idea they're trying to stick it to the guy no matter what."

"You think the army is out to get him? You don't think he's guilty?"

"Hell no! That guy is a gung-ho soldier. No way would he do anything to hurt our country."

"You seemed pretty upset with him when he ordered your wife and Linsey Curry to hand their reports to him."

"He should've listened to me. I knew he was a stickler for the rules, and I tried to warn him not to interfere with the procedure. He thought he was doing the right thing and look what it got him."

"What about you two? Why fudge reports?"

"Ho! Jenny didn't fudge anything. Those reports are subjective. It's all how you see it that affects your opinion. The so called objective parts are badly written and the way you check-off your answers depends on your interpretation of an ambiguous statement."

"What does that mean?"

"In one part you write down your own observation. The next part is composed of a list of statements and you can only check agree or disagree. This is not an exact science. All those damn missiles hit the target. How effectively they destroyed the target is what the reports are meant to determine."

"Then why change Linsey's report?"

"That damn bitch was out to get me. I dumped her when I met Jenny, but I would've gotten rid of her anyway; she was getting on my nerves. Always correcting my speech, telling me to stop swearing and don't go around unshaven. I knew that bitch was submitting mostly negative reports. That could result in the army asking for adjustments that were not needed. That would not help the army and certainly not my company. So I asked Jenny to correct the reports."

"But you did want the reports to be more favorable?"

"Hell no! I wanted accurate reports. Subjective, yes, but not slanted one way or the other. Jenny was pretty damn good in judging the performance of the missiles. Testing our missiles costs a fortune, and we at Aerodynamics don't have that type of R&D budget. We rely on the US Army tests to help fine tune our missiles.

The army helps us bring our products up to the standard at which they can purchase them."

"How come you weren't so positive about Matt at the trial?"

"I didn't want Linsey's reports with her negative bias to go through, and I wanted Matt to stay out of it."

"But you didn't tell the court you didn't think Matt was capable of handing those reports to the Russian."

"I couldn't. When Colonel Buckley asked me that, the prosecution objected, and the court upheld his objection. Like I said from what went on during the trial I'm sure the army was so sure of his guilt that they did not care what evidence Colonel Buckley introduced."

Jimmy came away from his visit to Toni and Jenny with the firm conviction that nether of the two had anything to do with the reports getting in the hands of the Russians. At the same time, he was more convinced than ever that he would find evidence to clear Matt, he just had to keep after new clues.

Before Jimmy had a change to dig into Matt's case any further in the hope of finding evidence that could clear him, he received shocking news. Helga had committed suicide. He decided to go to IEDC to gather more information surrounding the facts of her suicide. Before leaving for Austin, Texas, Jimmy made sure news of her death would be withheld from Matt.

Upon his arrival in Austin, Jimmy went directly to the headquarters of IEDC. There he met with Sam Stine the company CEO. Sam was on fire. "I'm moving this company out of this fucking country. They killed a wonderful human being. You never met her, but she was something else. A beauty with brains and one of the kindest gals you'd ever meet. She stayed away from men, but I still had a crush on her. If it wasn't for our age difference I would have made a serious pass at her."

It took forever for Sam to calm down, and it wasn't until he had finished his rant that Jimmy managed to introduce himself and explain that he was Matt's civilian lawyer. Jimmy told Sam why he had come to see him. "I'm working on his appeal. I want to go beyond showing that the flimsy circumstantial evidence presented was not enough to prove his guilt beyond a reasonable doubt. That should be enough for a reversal. But I am out to prove that somehow the two of them were framed. I'll need your help."

"You got it! Anything you need. My lawyers started working on Helga's case but they got no further than keeping her out of jail and getting her trial postponed until after the court martial. Now that she is dead, there most likely won't be a trial, and they'll just declare her guilty. Which is *Bullshit*! She loved this country. Here, look at the note she left us."

Sam handed Jimmy a copy of Helga's suicide note.

*Something evil has happened. The country
which I loved and worked hard for both in
peace times and war has betrayed my love
and my lover. Matt is not guilty!!!! I know
this, but they never let me explain. They
accused me of helping him commit an act
which he was incapable of. The only thing
Matt is guilty of is loyalty to the US Army
and his country and the only thing I'm
guilty of is loving him. I cannot and will
not live apart from Matt. Matt, I'll wait
for you in heaven.*

Jimmy could not help but become emotional upon
reading the note. He asked how Helga killed herself. "She
hung herself," Sam replied. He quickly added that he
would take care of her funeral. He would make sure the
funeral would not reflect the fact she had committed
suicide nor that she had been charged with espionage.

"They will not release her body to me, but her father
arrives this evening and I'll make arrangements with him.
He moved to Moscow after Helga's mother died. He re-
married ten years ago. His second wife is a French
newspaper correspondent. She and Helga did not get
along, and he has not seen his daughter in over four years."

Jimmy thought Helga's father might be helpful in
Matt's case. "I'd appreciate it if you introduce me to him.
Even though he has not seen Helga for a while, he might
have some idea why they are pointing the finger at his
daughter in this spy case. That information could help Matt
too."

Sam arranged for Jimmy to meet Helga's father at his office late the next day. When Jimmy entered Sam's office Mr. Kozlov was already there. Sam made a very formal introduction, but Helga's father waved it off. "We're in the United States now so please call me by my first name. It's Sasha."

Jimmy offered his condolences for Sasha's loss and assured him he had heard nothing but positive things about his daughter. After they exchanged a few pleasantries, they got right down to business. Sasha explained, "I wasn't very close to my daughter. I didn't even know about her involvement with Major Ramsey until after they arrested her. I did follow her career and knew more or less where she was stationed, but I know little about her personal life."

Sam interrupted him, "Your English is excellent."

"Why thank you. As a young man I attended the Russian language school. It was run by the KGB. Yes, at that time in my life I was a member of the communist party. Not only did it give me the opportunity to go to the language school, but I was able to get my daughter into a very good school. I can see the two of you giving each other a knowing look, but my having been a member of the party should not raise suspicion. I left the party more than twenty years ago. I was disillusioned when the party did not move Russia closer to the West. Besides Manon, my second wife, would not stand for it. She is French in heart and soul and has no use for communism."

Even though Sasha said he left the communist party a long time ago, Jimmy was sure that that was what led to the charges against Helga and Matt. "Have you ever been questioned about the case against your daughter?"

"No, nobody approached me on this matter. Like I said, I only heard about the case when she was arrested. At that time, I was refused a visa to come to the US to see her. She was not allowed to call me, and I couldn't contact her. I could've pulled a few strings, but there was a good reason for me not to."

Sam was curious. "And why might that be?"

"Not now. Maybe I can tell you later. But first I'd like to know if either of you can find out if my past membership in the Party had anything to do with the charges against the two of them?"

Sam and Jimmy answered at the same time. Both of them were sure they could find out. Sam would request the lawyers who had been working on Helga's behalf to dig into the government records to see if they could find any mention of Sasha's past. Jimmy was sure it was not part of the evidence the army presented during Matt's court martial. He planned to ask Colonel Buckley to petition the court to have additional records of the investigation released for the pending appeal.

Both were successful. When the three of them met three weeks later in Sam's office, Sasha exploded on hearing their reports. Their reports confirmed the fact that the government and the army had relied solely on Sasha's being a member of the communist party to prove that Matt had passed the test reports through Helga to her father who placed them in hands of his government.

Sasha was red in the face he was so angry, "Have they gone crazy! Who the hell did that sloppy research?

They should have known. If I'd known they did not use all the facts about me, I would have come immediately. I thought that based on my identity they would have quietly dropped the case. I did not know about Matt Ramsey, but identifying me should have helped him too."

"Who the hell are you?" Sam asked.

"Okay. They fucked up and killed my daughter and I'm no longer going to protect them."

Jimmy chimed in, "This makes no sense. Sasha who are you!"

"Manon and I are CIA contacts in Moscow. We've been supplying the US with information for years. When they were investigating my daughter, they should have found my CIA connection. My CIA connection would have eliminated me as the person who could be used by my daughter to pass the reports on to the Russians. That would have been enough to look for other culprits and not concentrate on Colonel Ramsey as the prime and only suspect. To stop looking after they noted my past Party membership amounts to criminal negligence.

"On hearing of Helga's arrest I was sure they would drop the case against her once the government identified me as a CIA agent. When this did not happen, I tried to go to the US to straighten things out. I had to be very discrete in revealing my CIA connection. If I was not careful, I could blow my cover and be in danger of being arrested by the Russian authorities. Worse than that I would have put Manon in danger. So I did not use my connections to get a visa. Instead I contacted my handler at the US Embassy to request that CIA headquarters in Langley step in and have the case dropped. By the time the proper information had gotten through and was verified, my daughter was dead. They killed her! I wasn't close to Helga, our relationship became strained after I married Manon. But I swear, they'll pay for this."

Jimmy was the first to speak. "Sasha I admire how composed you are. Under similar circumstances I would be threatening to shoot all those who screwed up. You're right; the army's not finding your CIA connection is criminal negligence if not much worse. But before we dig into who did what we should concentrate on getting your daughter's name cleared and the case against Matt reversed."

Sam agreed. "Yeah I would like to see Helga's name cleared as soon as possible. I don't know this fellow, Matt. But Helga sounded so happy when she called to tell me about him, that and for her sake I want him exonerated. Jimmy how do we do that?"

"The best way to remove any suspicion from the two of them is finding the actual perpetrator."

Sam agreed. "But how do we go about doing that?"

Sasha suggested letting the CIA handle it. Jimmy was opposed to that. "That might risk exposing you and we certainly want to keep Manon from accidently being outed. No, leave it to me. My firm deals with criminal investigation all the time. We'll find the real spy."

Chapter Two

From Austin, Jimmy went directly to see Matt. He was not in his cell and Jimmy had to contact Colonel Buckley to find out where he was. Colonel Buckley informed him that Matt had suffered a nervous breakdown and had been taken to a military hospital where he was confined to the criminal ward. Jimmy asked what led to Matt's breakdown. Colonel Buckley was hesitant to tell Jimmy the reason. He hemmed and hawed but final admitted that someone from the prosecution working on Matt's appeal had let it slip that Helga committed suicide.

Upon hearing this Jimmy exploded. "What more can they do to Matt? Have those incompetent assholes gone completely berserk? It's starting to look like a conspiracy against him." He demanded that Colonel Buckley meet him at the hospital as soon as possible.

When Jimmy entered Matt's hospital room, Matt was lying face down on his bed and did not respond to Jimmy's arrival. Jimmy turned to Colonel Buckley. "Why is he alone in this room, nobody watching him? I want you to contact whoever is in charge here and order a suicide watch."

When he did not get immediate action, Jimmy called his office and asked them to prepare a request for a court order. That lit a fire under the supervising staff and finally an around-the-clock watch was ordered. After he took care of that, Jimmy wanted to know what medical care Matt was getting. Colonel Buckley did not know so the two of them went to see the chief of staff of the hospital. She was very helpful and agreed to have a psychiatrist added to the medical team assigned to Matt's case.

Jimmy realized Matt was in no condition to talk to anyone about the appeal yet. He left the hospital and during the week that followed he called repeatedly to find out if there had been any improvement in Matt's condition. Progress was slow but there was some improvement. Jimmy planned to go and see Matt at the beginning of the next week.

Jimmy spent the week going over the reports of the investigators he had assigned to Matt's case. He was starting to get discouraged; none of the reports contained a positive lead. When he got to Walter Sellers' report things changed. Jimmy grabbed the phone and called Walt. "Walt I'm looking at the report you sent in yesterday. ...Yeah, that's major. Please come up to my office. We have to talk about this." When Walt arrived Jimmy was visibly excited. "You're sure about this? He bought a Corvette last month?"

"Yes. I've been checking on Specialist Joel Johnson for a while now. When I first started to widen my research on this guy, I saw that his credit rating was abysmal. I started digging and I've discovered a slew of debt. Lots of unpaid bills, credit cards maxed out; the guy was a financial mess. I say *was* because things have changed. You always tell us, 'follow the money.' Well, this guy is a prime suspect, so I stayed on him. Right after he returned from Iraq he started paying off his debts and getting rid of the balance on his credit cards. At first, I thought he must have gotten a lot of extra combat pay while over in Iraq, but that turned out not to be the case. I was in the middle of trying to find out where he was getting all that money from, when I discovered he buys a brand new Corvette. When I went to the dealer to find out how he financed the car, I was stonewalled. The manager would not go any further than to confirm that Johnson bought a top-of-the-line Corvette.

"I hung around the showroom for a while and found out which salesman made the sale. That salesman and I had a great dinner that night and I heard all about the deal. Mind you, he did not trade in his old pickup. He paid cash! He told the manager he didn't trust banks and always kept his savings at home in a special safe. The dealership reported this unusual transaction to their bank, and I assume that report is still floating around somewhere. Jimmy, I think we have our man."

Jimmy was delighted. "I think you're right, but we need more. What you found is great but it is all circumstantial. We need hard evidence, like proof the money came from Russian sources, or even better, proof he made copies of the reports and passed them on or had them passed on to Russian agents."

Walt was all fired up. "I'll get that! I'll hang the bastard. Tell that Colonel Ramsey of yours he's off the hook. Walt caught the traitor."

Jimmy felt a lot better than during his previous visit when he entered Matt's hospital room. He asked Colonel Buckley to step outside and take the orderly assigned to the suicide watch with him. "Colonel I want to talk to my client in private. I'm not impressed with how Matt's rights were protected while I was in Austin. No one from the prosecution should've been allowed to speak to him without you or Captain Pentowski being present. Colonel, you should've been able to prevent such a violation of his rights. I can use this in the appeal, but I don't think I'll need it."

After Colonel Buckley and the orderly left the room, Jimmy sat down next to Matt's bed. "The last time you lost a dear one I behaved terribly. This time is different; I'm on your side. Please trust me when I tell you I will find the bastard responsible for getting those reports in the hand of the Russians. I promise that both you and Helga will be cleared of any wrongdoing."

That caught Matt's attention. He turned around slowly and faced Jimmy. His speech was a little garbled so Jimmy suspected he'd been given strong doses of sedatives. "How can you promise that? They put a whole fucking case together to make it look like I did it."

Jimmy was happy that, despite the sedatives which were keeping him calm, Matt was quite lucid. "Yes, they did produce a strong circumstantial case, but they didn't have any actual proof. They couldn't produce any hard evidence because you did *not* do it."

"Thanks for believing so strongly in me. That does help. I'm very grateful that you stepped in and will represent me on appeal, but I'm worried. Actually, I don't care if I have to rot in jail, if only we could clear Helga." Matt paused and took a deep breath. "I can't bear the thought that I'll never see her again."

Jimmy was afraid Matt would break down again, but Matt composed himself and asked why Jimmy was so sure he could clear them. "In the first place, I know you could never do anything that would hurt this country. You have dedicated your life to the army, and betraying your country would go against everything you stand for. Secondly, I believe Helga might have been born in Russia but I am positive she liked the US better."

That almost brought a smile to Matt's face. "And that's going to be the basis of our appeal?"

"No, I said I would unmask the person or persons who handed over the test reports."

"I want to believe that. But how?"

"Matt, I've got a silver bullet, but there are things a lawyer can't tell. Not even to his client. Just trust me."

"If all you do is clear Helga, I'll love you forever. During our relationship I was surprised to find out that she was a religious person. Even if somehow you can clear her name, because of her suicide, we can't change the fact that she did not have a church burial."

"Who the hell told you she did not receive a proper church burial?"

"Nobody. I've just been lying here feeling guilty about that."

"Well you can stop feeling guilty about that. Helga was buried in a Catholic cemetery. It was a beautiful ceremony presided over by the local Catholic priest."

Matt could not really believe that. He was sure Jimmy said it to make him feel better. "I know you mean well, but Jimmy I know that can't be true."

"Damn it, Matt. It is!"

"How is that possible?"

"To understand that you have to know Sam Stine. Sam is the CEO of IEDC and makes it his business to know all about his employees. Sam knew that Helga was

Catholic and that her suicide would cause problems in arranging her funeral. He spoke to the local priest about it. The priest told Sam that The official _Catechism of the Catholic Church_ indicated that the person who committed suicide may not always be fully right in their mind; and thus not one-hundred-percent morally culpable: 'Grave psychological disturbances, anguish, or grave fear of hardship, suffering, or torture can diminish the responsibility of the one committing suicide.' The Catholic Church prays for those who have committed suicide, knowing that Christ shall judge the deceased fairly and justly.

"Sam contacted an old buddy of his, the chief of police. The chief just happened to be a good friend of the coroner. The coroner's report eventually showed that Helga had fallen off a stool while getting a bottle from the top shelf in her kitchen. The fall broke her neck, and she died instantly. The suicide note mysteriously disappeared."

Chapter Three

Jimmy instructed Walter Seller to arrange a meeting with the CIA. "I want to meet with an agent, but it can't be at a CIA office or mine. I don't want to tip off anyone that the CIA is involved in Lieutenant Colonel Ramsey's case."

Walter arranged a meeting in an out of the way restaurant in Fredericksburg, Virginia. During the meeting Jimmy gave the CIA agent all the details of Matt's case including all that Walter had discovered about Joel Johnson. "The CIA can't get openly involved. We can't risk exposing Helga's father or his wife. Their connection to the CIA needs to stay out of all this. Once we show it was Johnson who copied and passed the reports to a Russian agent, Helga's affair with Matt becomes irrelevant, and her father stays out of the picture.

"My plan calls for Walter and me to go to Iraq and sniff around to see if we can come up any contacts Johnson had who could have been the ones to help him contact Russian agents. We'll need papers identifying us as newspaper correspondents working on a story about the Peshmerga helping in the fight against ISIS. The CIA should be able to get these papers for us."

The CIA had no trouble securing the proper identification papers for Jimmy and Walter. They left for Iraq a few days after they received those papers and an authorization to visit military facilities. On arrival in Iraq, they went directly to Centri 4 to interview the local Peshmerga commander. At the gate they identified themselves as newspaper correspondents. Before they were allowed to enter Centri 4 they had to show documents from the US Army authorizing them to interview U.S. military personnel and members of the Peshmerga. This authorization was verified by a call to the US Command in Bagdad.

Upon entering the commander's office they could not hide their surprise; the local commander of the Peshmerga was a female. Ronahi got up from behind her desk to greet them. She was all business and looked them over with a hard stare. "Welcome to Centri 4. I have been informed you're here to do a story on the Kurds' involvement in the fight against ISIS?"

Jimmy complemented her on her English. Her response to this rather patronizing remark was cold and haughty. "Thank you. Most Kurds speak several languages. That's what happens when you're spread out over four countries and don't have one of your own."

Jimmy continued, "We would like to concentrate on a specific period. The time when Lieutenant Colonel Matt Ramsey was stationed here in Centri 4. Did you know him?"

"Of course. Matt was a major for most of the time he served here. He was a good friend to us Kurds. We've heard rumors of what the U.S. Army has done to him and we are very angry. Have you come here to do a story about that?"

Walter glanced at Jimmy wondering how he would respond. Jimmy sensed he could trust this young woman and that she could help them. "We're angry too, and the truth is we're here to try and help him. We want to find out what really happened. We know Colonel Ramsey didn't do what he's accused of."

"I was here, but not in command when Colonel Matt was here. If you want details from someone who knew him very well, you have to talk to my husband."

"Your husband?"

"Yes my husband. Agrin Sivan was the Kurdish commander when Colonel Matt served with us. My husband was badly wounded, and Matt saved his life."

"Where can we meet him?"

"I'll be glad to take you. He's in Irbil."

They entered a modest house near the center of town. Ronahi had called ahead. Agrin was waiting for them in a wheelchair in the living room. After pleasantries were exchanged, an elderly woman brought out a huge tray of cakes and sweets and started pouring tea for everybody. Agrin waved at the tray, "Please help yourself; it's our custom to make visitors welcome. And you are double welcome; I heard you've come to help my friend, Colonel Matt."

"We're hoping to find some information that will prove he isn't guilty."

Agrin flew into a rage. "They're crazy! He's an excellent soldier, a hero. He would never betray his country. Some traitor must have done what he's accused of. They're trying to pin it on him because he saved my life. His big crime was getting me to the hospital pretending I was an American. The cruel joke is I *am* an American and he *knew* that. I was born in your fucking country."

Jimmy waited till Agrin calmed down before he spoke. "That was Matt's initial impression too. But it was his relationship with Helga Kozlov, who is Russian, that made them point the finger at him."

This time Agrin really lost it. He practically screamed, "Helga is a fine lady! How dare they?"

Jimmy didn't have the heart to tell Agrin that Helga was dead. He quickly changed the subject. "You might as well know. I'm not a journalist; I'm Matt's lawyer. I can't say too much. Enough said, we think we know who passed the reports to the Russians, and it definitely wasn't Matt. Before I left for Iraq, I was briefed by Matt's appointed lawyers. The U.S. Army is aware that the Kurds knew a new weapon was being tested and reports about these tests got into the hands of the Russians. So I can speak freely with you. As I said, we know for sure Matt did not hand over the reports. It's my job to prove who did it."

Ronahi had been following the conversation. She didn't say anything until Agrin calmed down. She said she had heard a lot about Helga, but didn't get to know her until Helga was staying in Matt's room on the base. Ronahi explained that at that time Agrin was still in command. He had put Ronahi in charge of the Kurds stationed on Centri 4. Helga was very worried about Matt. The battle for Mosul was raging and Helga knew Matt was involved. She relied on Ronahi to keep her informed. The two of them had talked a lot, and it was clear Helga cared deeply for Matt. Ronahi stressed that Helga was in love with Matt and would never betray him by passing secrets to the Russians or even encourage him to do so. Ronahi went on to explain that when Agrin was wounded it was

Helga who comforted her. Ronahi wasn't married to Agrin then, but Helga sensed she was in love with him and helped her get information on his condition.

Walter smiled at Ronahi. Now that he had seen the softer side of this young woman, he liked her a lot better. "Ronahi, let me ask you, did anyone from the U.S. military ask you questions about Helga?"

"What type of questions?"

"Anything. Like about her job, who she was friendly with, or that she was Russian."

"The only person who asked me about Helga, and also about Matt, was a man named Leo Muller. He was not in uniform. He said he was from Military Intelligence and he had a badge."

"What did he ask?"

"Mostly about Matt's relationship with Helga. How often they saw each other and things like that. Some of his questions made me feel uneasy."

"How so?"

"Well they were about…you know…sexual things."

Jimmy jumped in, "Explain please."

Before Ronahi could continue Agrin stopped her. "My wife will not discuss such things. That man Leo Muller had no manners! You don't ask Kurdish women such things. I hate that guy! He prevented me from going to the US to help Matt."

That intrigued Jimmy. "Tell us about that."

"When I was in the American hospital, I heard about Matt's arrest. As soon as I was able to travel, I wanted to go to the US to help Matt. I wanted to tell that stupid government of yours that Matt was a very loyal soldier and would never do anything to hurt his country."

Walter didn't like what he heard. "You hate Americans?"

"Hell no. Only the government. They've never been on the side of the Kurds. Look how long it took for them to give us the weapons we needed. And I despise stupid idiots like that guy Muller. I like American people. I loved Matt even before he saved my live. And those guys who flew the chopper into the combat zone to come and get me . . . I'm grateful to those wonderful doctors who worked hard to keep me alive, despite the fact the army didn't want them to treat a Kurdish fighter."

Jimmy didn't like Walter distracting Agrin. He was keeping him from telling more about Leo Muller. "Please get back to Agent Muller. How did he stop you from going to America?"

"I'm born in the US but don't have an American passport. So I needed a visa. I was part of the Peshmerga and apparently MI had to clear me. Muller blocked my clearance. I bet that same bastard told the army Matt was the guilty one."

Jimmy looked at Walter. "I think it's time to pay a visit to this mysterious Agent Muller.

Chapter Four

Agent Muller's office was tucked away in a nondescript building in the middle of Baghdad. The CIA had arranged an official message informing him that Jimmy McDowell and Walter Sellers, reporters for the Washington Post, were working on a background story about the court martial of Lieutenant Colonel Matthaeus Ramsey. Agent Muller was requested to give the reporters his full cooperation. The government was aware the court martial proceeding had disclosed facts that might have been secret before.

Agent Muller was sitting behind a desk stacked high with paper binders sloppily marked with a dossier name and number. To his left was a low table with three empty diet coke cans and a white Styrofoam container, the remains of his take-out lunch. "So, you guys are doing a story on that traitor Ramsey."

"Actually, no. We're hoping to piece a story together on how he was caught."

"Well, that's easy enough."

"Really? How's that?"

"You're looking at the guy who caught him."

"Wow! Can you tell us how you managed to catch him? What put you on him in the first place? Did you have any help?"

"Nah, no help. I figured it out by myself. It's my job to keep track of what goes on in this command. I'm way ahead of the other MI guys; I make it my business to know what every swinging dick in my area is up to."

"You have a dossier on every military person serving here?"

"That would be going too far, but this one was obvious. The guy was having a hot affair with a Russian chick. When a report came through that the Ruskies had some of our secret reports, I started checking were these reports originated. And bingo! They came from a unit under the command of the same fellow screwing that Russian babe. Naturally, I checked out that gal. When she started at IEDC she obtained Limited Access Authorization (LAA). Once she got her green card, she obtained more access to jobs that require security clearance. Both times her background check revealed that her father in Russia was a member of the communist party. For some reason not revealed in the report, this was waived."

Jimmy waived for Muller to stop. "Did you ever check why this was waived?"

"Hell no. Why should I? She has a green card, but never becomes a U.S. citizen. Her father is a communist. What more do I need to know? The Ruskies cleverly plant an agent in a sensitive area. You might have heard, she's quite a piece of ass. She easily seduced a guy who had access to sensitive information. Knowing all that, I didn't need to be a rocket scientist to figure out how the Ruskies got our reports."

"And that's the report you submitted to the army?"

Muller laughed. "It's not that simple. I reported my findings to my boss. From there it was passed to U.S. Army Intelligence and Security Command - INSCOM. Next thing I know Matthaeus is arrested and sent back to the U.S. I was hoping for a promotion, but nothing has come through."

After Muller finished his account, Jimmy and Walter stayed a while to make small talk. Muller did his best to show them how important his job was. They were not impressed; his telephone never rang and he didn't seem to have any other matters on his agenda for the rest of the afternoon. They finally got away by making up a phony story about having to meet with another journalist assigned to a story about the Iraqi 1st Commando Battalion, part of the 1st Special Operations Brigade.

As soon as they left agent Muller's office Jimmy and Walter headed back to Irbil to meet with Agrin.

Chapter Five

"Agrin have you ever heard of a US soldier named Johnson? Joel Johnson stationed on the same base as you?"

"Yes…he's a bad person."

Jimmy's eyes lit up and he took over the questioning. "What do you mean by bad person?"

"Oh, just not of good character."

"And that means?"

"Like I said he was not a nice man. He did not have good morals." Jimmy was getting impatient. Agrin was holding back something and by the look on Jimmy's face, he suspected that. Finally, Agrin said, "He did not respect our traditions."

Ronahi became irritated with Agrin's reluctance to tell Jimmy what he knew about Joel Johnson. "My husband didn't like Johnson's association with a woman named Benden. She is a Kurdish woman and we're ashamed of her behavior."

Walter was not afraid to ask about Benden's behavior. Agrin replied curly, "She's a whore."

Walter had to laugh. "No biggie. That's the oldest profession, and American soldiers have made use of their services no matter where they were stationed. That certainly is no reflection on you."

Agrin shot back, "It is! She's a Kurdish woman."

Walter realized he was on thin ice. "Oops. Sorry, I understand."

Jimmy felt it might be useful to talk to this woman, Benden. "I'd like to speak with Benden. Can you arrange for us to meet her?"

Ronahi offered to take them to see Benden, but before Jimmy could thank her for the offer, Agrin said, "No you won't."

Ronahi looked at Agrin and waited till their eyes met. "Agrin I love you very much, and you're my husband. But you're not my master. I will take these gentlemen to see Benden. I, too, am deeply ashamed of her behavior, but as a Kurdish woman, I know it's more important to repay our debt than to worry about this woman's immoral behavior. Colonel Matt saved your life, and we must help these gentlemen clear his name. I will not embarrass you by refusing to help repay your debt to your friend."

On the way to Benden's house, Jimmy asked. "Ronahi is Agrin angry with you? He did not want you to take us to Benden."

"You misunderstood. He's not angry. As a devout Muslim, he needed an excuse to recognize the existence of a woman like Benden. I gave him that excuse; he respects my opinion. I'm his wife, but more important I'm a military officer like him."

They arrived at a rather dismal looking house on what was clearly the wrong side of the tracks. Ronahi said she would not come in with them, but Benden had been informed that they were coming to see her. Jimmy knocked on the door and a fortyish woman opened. She was wearing a skin tight skirt which closely followed the slightly overweight curves of her body. "Someone called to say you were coming. If you're here for business, I don't do two at a time."

"No ma'am, we're here to talk to you about an American soldier you might know."

"I don't talk about my business. Goodbye!"

"Not so fast. Please let us explain. All we want to know is did you know a soldier named Joel Johnson?"

"That bastard? Yes. I hope he's dead."

"Wow! That's pretty harsh. Please tell us why you don't like him."

"And who are you?"

"We're from the US, and we think he's done some very bad things and should be punished."

On hearing they were interested in punishing Johnson, Benden's attitude changed. She invited Jimmy and Walter in and led them to a surprisingly well-furnished living room. When the three of them were seated she said. "My American customers don't call me Benden; they call me Bunny."

Walter complemented her on the name. "That's a nice name. They must like you. Do you have many American friends, *eh* customers?"

"I don't think I have to tell you."

Jimmy was afraid she'd clam up and responded quickly. "Of course not. Just tell us about Joel Johnson. How did you meet him?"

"The usual way. I picked him up in a local bar. He was by himself and the bartender pointed at me when he asked for a certain type of woman. He bought me a drink, and soon after we headed to my house. Here in the living room we became friendly and, as is my custom, I let him play with my breasts to warm him up. He got excited, but I told him he'd have to pay before we could go into the bedroom. When I told him my price was two hundred dollars, he was surprised. He said that was too much for him. Could I do a quickie for less? I told him no. I only do all night for two hundred. He begged and pulled out fifty bucks, but I said no and told him to get out.

"I didn't see him for more than three weeks. Then he showed up in the same bar and waved two hundred dollar bills in my face. Same routine, we went here to the house. He gave me the two hundred dollars and wanted to go directly into my bedroom. He undressed quickly and sat on the bed. I undressed slowly to get him nice and hot. When I approached the bed, he grabbed me by my hair and pulled my face into his crotch.

"I screamed, 'No, I don't do that. Two hundred dollars is to fuck me regular way.' He did not listen and pulled me down real hard. I tried to pull away, but he held my hair real tight. He slapped my face real hard and said, 'You'll do what I want you bitch. I paid two hundred bucks and want a blow job. Now do it!' I tried to pull away as hard as I could. I punched him with both fists. He laughed, 'You want to box; I'll show you box.' He hit me hard, his punch landed between my nose and my eye. It hurt terribly and I was crying it hurt so bad. He seemed to enjoy seeing me cry. 'I'll knock your teeth out, so you can better suck my dick bitch.' Because I was yelling my mouth was open, and he forced his penis in."

Jimmy had heard enough. "Stop! Stop! I've heard enough. We get the picture."

Benden continued anyway. "The bastard. He didn't let me get out of the way when he came. Disgusting! I ran to rinse my mouth and he just sat there and grinned. I should've bitten down hard on his dick, but this was all new to me and I was terrified. The bastard might have had AIDS!"

"Did you call the police?"

"Come on, get serious. How can I call the police? They've been trying to arrest me for years. I couldn't even tell anyone; they would say I deserved it."

"What did you do?"

"I threw his clothes at him and told him he had three minutes to get out. I'm pretty strong and I'm sure he believed me when I told him I'd scratch his eyes out."

"Do you know how he got the two hundred dollars? Apparently, he did not have that much before. Maybe this was after payday?"

"I know about payday. That's my busy time. But this had nothing to do with payday."

"How can you be sure?"

"I said I couldn't tell anyone, but that is not true. I pay bartenders for any clients they send my way. I told Jorin. He is the bartender who told Johnson I was what you guys call a call girl. Well, Jorin told me Johnson had plenty cash after he became friends with a man named Akeem Kattan."

"Do you know where we can find this Akeem Kattan?"

"No idea. A while back I tried to pick him up in the Lagoon, an upscale bar I usually don't work in. He turned me down flat and threatened to have me thrown out for soliciting."

"Did he know about your run in with Johnson?"

"Who knows? You could ask Jorin; he knows everything about everybody."

Chapter Six

They found Jorin in the Euro Club. The bar was packed and they had to ask around to find him. They finally located him behind the main bar directly in front of the dance floor. They ordered drinks from his assistant and asked if Jorin could come over to talk to them. It took a while, but he finally came over. "You guys want something special?"

"We need some information and are willing to pay for it."

Jorin laughed. "Don't worry; info about popular ladies is free. Can't give you my personal reference, but getting you hooked up is free."

"Thanks, but we don't need you to hook us up with some girls. We need some information on a guy."

"Sorry. I don't go there. Boy - girl, I don't go beyond that. Sorry."

Jorin turned away. Jimmy stopped him. "Misunderstanding. We need information about a man to find out about his background. No more than that. Benden said you can help us. It might help get revenge for what happened to the poor girl."

"You know what happened to Benden? What that creep Johnson did to her?"

"Yes we know all about that."

"Unfortunately, I can't help you. He's no longer in Iraq. All I know is he was stationed in a nearby base called Centri 4. They have Kurds and Americans stationed there.

He left suddenly; I don't know why. A whole bunch of them left at the same time."

"We're looking for information about that Johnson fellow, but we're more interested in his friend Akeem Kattan."

Jorin looked around the room. "Take a seat all the way in back of this room. As soon as I can find someone to sub for me at the bar, I'll join you."

Jimmy and Walter found an empty table against the back wall. The music in the bar was very loud but in the back it was less noisy than at the bar.

Before long, Jorin joined them. "Why are you interested in Akeem Kattan. Are you CIA or US military intelligence?"

Jimmy decided it would be best if they played it straight with Jorin without blowing their true identity. "Neither. We're newspaper guys working on a story about the trial of Lieutenant Colonel Ramsey. Did you hear about that case?"

"Of course. Things like that can't be kept secret here in Iraq. What is not widely known is that the Kurds in the area don't agree with what is happening to Colonel Ramsey. Especially the officers of the Peshmerga; they don't think Ramsey is guilty. The guy was amazingly popular while serving here."

"That's why we want to get the full story and we have to find out more about this Akeem Kattan."

"How the hell do you think he fits in? He's a bad guy, that's for sure, but how does he fit in. Did this Ramsey fellow know him?"

"No. We don't think so. We think there may be a connection through that creepy guy Johnson. What do you know about the connection between the two of them?"

"Yes, the two creeps were friends. I don't know much about Johnson beyond what he did to Benden. Before I pointed Johnson in the direction of Benden, I hardly ever saw him here in the bar. After that, he must have become friends with Akeem Kattan because they were often in here together. Kattan always picked up the check, even though Johnson liked to flash the roll of cash he carried."

"What makes you call Kattan a creep?"

Jorin looked around; making sure no one could hear what he had to say. "A year ago he showed up here in Irbil. No one knows where he came from or why he settled here in Irbil. He has no visible means of support; nothing in the way of a job, but he always has plenty of cash. There have been all sorts of rumors about him. The one I've heard most is that he is part of a gang involved in human trafficking. We guard our girls and young women carefully. There have been no incidents of any one going missing. Recently, I have heard something new. I don't know anyone who has been approached, but I have heard from several sources that he has offered money for information on troop movement and strength."

Jimmy could hardly contain himself from jumping up and yelling *Bingo!* "Do you think Johnson was feeding him that information?"

"That's possible."

Jimmy leaned over the table and stared at Jorin. That made Jorin uneasy. "What's the matter? Did I say anything wrong?"

"On the contrary. I have to know how much you hate Johnson. Do you hate him enough to see him convicted of the crime Matt Ramsey is accused of?"

"I despise him for what he did to Benden. Let me tell you about that poor gal. Most of her family was killed when Hussain bombed us Kurds. As a small girl she learned to fend for herself. As a young woman, that became easier. There were plenty of American and allied soldiers who were willing to pay big money for the sexual favors of a pretty young woman. Then all these soldiers left and the locals shunned her. The ones who condemned her the most secretly paid a couple of bucks to have intercourse with her. She just about starved to death until foreigners returned and she could more or less openly practice the only trade she knows. She pays me for every guy I send her way. What she does not know is that I bought the house she lives in. I told her she inherited it as the only surviving relative of a distant cousin. Oh yes, the furniture came with it. I had it put in just before she took possession."

Walter shook his head. "Poor gal didn't deserve what that creep did to her."

"I don't think you really understand how traumatic it was for her. All of us know about AIDS and how it is transmitted. Every one of the women here who offer sex either for free or for pay are told never allow a strange guy to enter their vagina without a condom. And never ever allow them to put their penis in your mouth or your backside. That could mean a death sentence. Benden thought Johnson might have had AIDS and was trying to kill her. When she told me about what he did, I took her to the hospital to have her tested. She tested clean, but that did not remove the fear she felt."

Jimmy took a deep breath. "I'm hearing a lot of things I would've liked to skip, but now I have something you will like to hear. I'm not a newspaper reporter. I'm Matt Ramsey's lawyer; I'm going to clear Matt from all charges by hanging that bastard Johnson. And you can help."

"I want to help. What can I do?"

"Come to America and tell the court about the relationship between Johnson and Kattan. Not what others said but what you personally observed."

"When can I come?"

"As soon as I let you know that I have proof who Kattan is working for and who is supplying his money."

After they exchanged address and phone information, Jorin returned to the bar. Jimmy and Walter ordered another round of drinks before they went back to their hotel.

Early the next morning they took a taxi to Agrin's house. As a habit drilled into him during his military career, Agrin was up early. "I understand you had to see that woman, but please don't bring her into my house."

"No, we did not bring her along. But she was very helpful. We have collected a lot of information, but we need one more piece that will be vital in the case against Joel Johnson."

"And what might that be?"

"We need more information about Kattan and we need your help to get it for us."

"How do you expect me to do that?"

"Agrin, do the Kurds have their own CIA or something like it?"

"Maybe yes and maybe no."

"Actually, I don't give a damn how you get us the information. You have enough influence to order around the clock surveillance of a man named Akeem Kattan."

"Don't have to. We've already have him on our radar. We suspect him of human trafficking."

"Wrong. In some way we think he's an agent for the Russian government."

"What makes you think that?"

"Simple. Out of nowhere, Johnson gets a lot of money. Kattan has lots of money, and he befriended Johnson. Johnson had full access to the reports that wound up in Russian hands. Do you need a road map, or can you take it from here?"

"Is there anyone else you suspect of taking the documents?"

"Everyone else we suspected has been cleared. Now all evidence points to Johnson. I have no doubt he did it, but I need to show how he got those reports to the Russians."

"How long do we have to come up with something?"

"As long as it takes to give me incontestable evidence that Johnson passed those reports via Kattan to the Russians."

"Will you stick around till we find something?"

"No. We'll be going back to the States tomorrow. You'll pass on all the information to a man named Jorin. I'm sure you know him. He will hand carry the information to us. When Johnson's trial starts, I'll let you know who we need to come and testify."

Chapter Seven

Matt's appeal was starting in five weeks and Jimmy had not heard from Agrin or Jorin. He decided to wait one more week before returning to Iraq to personally find out what was going on. He had already booked his flight when an unannounced visitor walked into his office. "Hello Jimmy. Boy, that's a long trip from Irbil to here."

"Jorin! You didn't tell me you were coming. I would have picked you up from the airport."

"You said no telephone conversation, just bring you the report. So here I am."

"Is it a good report? Can we use it?"

"Would I make this long trip for nothing? It's a great report. Those guys really know their stuff. You won't believe what they found out."

Jimmy grabbed the thick envelop Jorin was holding and hastily started skimming through the report. The more he read, the more excited he got. The report started by detailing all the visitors to Akeem Kattan's apartment. Kattan made it abundantly clear that he had many girlfriends. The Kurdish agents were not fooled, and they zeroed in on one particular girl. This woman, Dina Abdulin, traveled a lot. She claimed to work for a promotional company which had major hotel chains as clients. She traveled to many European cities, but each time she went to Austria she wound up visiting the Russian Embassy in Vienna. The Kurds had managed to tap into her cell phone but she was extremely careful and avoided any compromising calls. Next, they slipped into her hotel room in London and installed a remote-controlled recording device in the lining of her briefcase. That did it. They recorded everything that happened during her next visit to the Russian Embassy in Vienna.

Turns out she was not only the handler for Kattan - she was also the contact person for several other Russian agents spread out over Europe. The recording revealed the names of couriers who, wearing specially tailored clothing, distributed cash to the Russian agents under her control.

Jimmy put down the report and thanked Jorin for personally bringing it. "This is great. There's enough here to reverse Matt's case on appeal and hang that son of a bitch Johnson."

"Not so fast Jimmy. They dug up some great stuff, but you can't use the report till we say so."

"Who's we?"

"Don't really know. Agrin gave me this report. He arranged for my visa and instructed me to hand carry it to you. He also gave me a message which I was to orally give you."

"And what was that?"

"Like I said, you can't use the report until you hear from me that it is okay."

"But Matt's appeal is coming up in less than two weeks and we have to make sure Johnson doesn't slip through our fingers."

"Johnson won't get away. He has been arrested for sexual assault."

"He's what?"

"I told you Benden couldn't go to the police to report what Johnson did to her. Well, she got some help from some influential persons and filed a report. The police looked into her complaint. I testified that she and Johnson were in the bar on the night she claimed he assaulted her. I saw them leave together. The police report supported her claim that Johnson forced her to perform a sexual act against her will. The report was given to General Edelman in Baghdad. Johnson was arrested here in the US to stand trial for assault while he was stationed in Iraq."

"That's great, but what about Matt's appeal? I need the report to help clear him."

"Agrin told me he understands your concern, but you can't use the report until the connection between Kattan and Russian agents is firmly established."

"If the appeal is denied, Matt will be sent to a place like Fort Leavenworth."

"No he won't. Agrin assured me he won't. He told me to tell you he's made sure his friend will be held in a friendly place until this whole thing is cleared up."

"I wish I could believe that. How the hell can Agrin control that?"

"Don't underestimate Agrin. He's very well connected. I'm learning about the connections between all those international organizations. I'm surprised they haven't caught Akeem Kattan in their web before. I'm not supposed to tell you . . . but they're going to use me to catch him."

PART THREE

Jorin

Chapter One

The day after Jorin arrived back in Iraq a man named Yamyl approached him. He came straight to the point. "I'm told you're willing to cooperate with us."

Jorin knew what the man meant, but he had to make sure he wasn't being led into a trap. "Can you identify yourself?"

"Someone will come to your bar tomorrow and give you clearance to deal with me."

The next day, just as the bar was closing, Benden came in. She signaled Jorin that she wanted to talk to him. He moved to the far end of the bar and leaned over so no one could hear what Benden had to say. "I have no idea what this is all about, but Ronahi came to my house and asked me to tell you Yamyl is okay. You can work with him."

Jorin realized that cooperating with Yamyl was not without danger. He was asked to befriend Akeem Kattan and wear a wire during every conversation he had with Kattan. The idea was for Jorin to be jealous of how much money Kattan had and all the girlfriends he probably slept with on a regular basis. Jorin barely survived on his salary, and if it weren't for generous tips from guys like Kattan, he wouldn't be able to afford his apartment.

It took a long time for Jorin to get into more than just a casual conversation with Kattan. Finally, Jorin saw him sitting by himself and he sat down to have a drink with him. Kattan's overblown ego made conversation easy. Jorin played along waiting for an opening. That came when Kattan asked how friendly he was with military personnel frequenting the bar. Jorin responded he knew most of them. He joked about the saying that people tell the bartender things they wouldn't tell their doctor. Kattan took the bait.

"They tell you things about their unit? Like maneuvers they will be going on and new things happening on post?"

"Yup. You name it; I've got to hear all about it and pretend I'm interested."

"Did you know information is worth money? It could be better than tips."

"I've heard that, but for me it's often instead of a tip. The attitude of the military types is often, 'You're my friend now, so I don't have to tip you.'"

"We could fix that."

"Oh sure. I could put up a sign telling them how much I charge per hour for leaning on my shoulder."

"No seriously. I can help you get some extra cash. Good information is worth lots of cash. Interested?"

"Of course. I can always use some extra money."

The two of them agreed Jorin would keep Kattan posted on any information he got from talking to military personnel. Kattan would let him know if the information was worth any money."

Jorin reported this development to Yamyl who promised to supply Jorin with sellable information. That worried Jorin. "I'm not about to hand the guy any actual information that would be valuable to the Russians."

"Don't worry. What we're doing is fully controlled by persons charged with protecting the security of the US and her allies. First, we'll hand you perfectly true information that is already known to the other side. To keep you interested, they'll pay you small bucks for that. Then we'll proceed to valuable stuff. It will be new to them, and they'll liberally reward you."

"You mean I'll be handing over real secret information? I'll be a spy!"

"Yes; you're a double agent. You've been one since you agreed to work with me. I hope you're not pulling back."

"I want to work with you guys. I trust Agrin, and he says you're okay. But I don't want to hand over information that will be useful to the wrong people."

"That can't be helped. It's all part of the game; you have to give up something to get something better in return. In this case, we'll be handing over information that can be used against us in order to trap one of their agents."

After the forth exchange, Kattan had great news. "Up to now I've only been able to get small amounts for you, but this time you had some real nice stuff. My contacts liked it a lot. Next week I'll bring you lots of cash."

Jorin was excited. Not because he was getting a lot of money; he knew he had set the trap and caught Kattan.

"We can't do that here. Can you come to my apartment with the cash?"

"Sure, give me your address."

Jorin gave Kattan the address of his apartment and asked him to meet him there after the bar closed on Friday night.

Kattan ran the bell at two-thirty Saturday morning. The bar normally closed at one and Jorin had been expecting him for the past hour. Kattan was carrying two long, narrow canvas bags that looked like they had been designed to be worn under one's coat. He was in a jovial mood and, with a big flourish, dumped the contents of the bags on the coffee table in the living room. Stacks of dollar bills fell all over the place.

There was a slight noise coming from the bedroom. Kattan looked up as the bedroom door opened and two armed men came into the living room. From the kitchen a woman appeared; she pointed a pistol at Kattan as she quickly moved to block the front door.

Kattan looked frightened. "Jorin what the hell is this? A robbery, but why? I'm giving you this cash why the guns; who are these people?"

The woman at the door spoke first. "A robbery. You should be so lucky. We're working with Interpol, the Iraqi secret service and other agencies. You are under arrest."

"What the hell for?"

"You're on Iraqi soil collecting information for a foreign country. Iraq has been requested to extradite you to the country whose documents you have stolen."

PART FOUR

Matt Ramsey continued

Chapter One

The taxi dropped Jimmy McDowell and his wife Suzie off in front of Le Bon Michel. It was raining so the doorman held up his umbrella while they entered the famous restaurant. Inside the Maître d' recognized Jimmy. "So nice to see you again Mr. McDowell. Hello, ma'am. I've reserved your favorite table for you; far away from the music."

Jimmy had to smile. He often entertained clients in this restaurant, and the Maître d' knew he hated it when the music interrupted his business discussions. "Thank you, Frederick. Tonight, it's not business. We're here to celebrate the wonderful outcome of the trial of our guest who should be arriving shortly."

Forty minutes passed and Matt had not arrived. Jimmy was getting worried and told Suzie he was going to the lobby to make a call. As he was getting up, he noticed a commotion in the front of the restaurant.

A slightly disheveled man was arguing with the Maître d'. It took Jimmy a few seconds to realize that it was Matt. He rushed over. "I'm so sorry Frederick; he's not dressed properly, but he's my guest. Please let me take him to my table."

"But of course, Mr. McDowell. I apologize; I didn't know the gentleman was your guest. I should have inquired."

The Maître d' turned to Matt. "I'm so sorry, sir. My fault. May I bring you a jacket?"

Jimmy answered, "That would be very nice Frederick. You had no way of knowing, thank you for your understanding."

Frederick brought the jacket to the table and helped Matt put it on. He was still worried about refusing entry to Jimmy's guest, and he offered Matt a drink to make up for the misunderstanding.

A waiter brought Matt the drink he selected, and Jimmy slipped a fifty dollar bill in Frederick's pocket to thank the Maître d' for ignoring the restaurant's strict dress code.

Suzie turned to Matt. "What's the matter Matt? You look like hell. You're completely vindicated, and that traitor Johnson will rot in jail. You should be on top of the world."

"Yeah that's great, but it doesn't bring Helga back."

"No it doesn't, but at least she was completely cleared of any involvement too."

Jimmy joined the conversation. "I've asked myself a million times if I had given the information I had immediately to her lawyers would it have prevented her death?"

Matt shook his head. "No, the army killed her."

Suzie didn't like where this was going. "Stop it both of you! One rotten guy in the Military Police is responsible for the horrible mess. Neither the army or Jimmy can be blamed for what happened."

Matt was not about to let go. "There was no basis for the army to pin things on me. Shit, you don't treat a decorated soldier that way!"

"They did try to make it up to you. If you had been willing to stay in the service, they planned to make you a full colonel immediately."

Jimmy reminded Matt that General Edelman, who was now a four-star general, personally came to see Matt to offer him the promotion and the chance to serve on his staff in D.C.

Matt waved off that argument. "It was easy to make nice when it was all over. Where was he when I needed him? He knew me; he must have known I could never betray my country no matter what. No, I want no part of the army; never again."

Suzie was concerned. "You can't just sit around and mourn. I never had a chance to meet Helga, but I'm sure she would expect better from you."

Jimmy agreed with his wife. "Rather than mourn Helga, do something we can remember her by."

Matt sneered. "Oh sure, go do something; but what? All I know is the army."

Jimmy had an idea and he became very animated. "Wrong! You have an engineering degree and we can build on that. You're going to work for IEDC and do what Helga was doing. That should honor her memory!"

"I can't. I don't have the training to do that sort of work."

"They'll train you. I'm sure Sam Stine will be happy to have you."

"No way."

"Damn it! Yes, way. I'm calling him in the morning."

Chapter Two

On his first day on the job at IEDC in Austin, Texas, Sam Stine the president took Matt to see Maya Karlsson. "Matt I want you to meet Maya. Maya joined the company way back in what I like to call the dark ages. She started as a management trainee and quickly became my private secretary. When I realized she knew more about the company than I did, I promoted her to vice-president, and now she is our chief operating officer. I have told Maya all about you and she has agreed to take it upon herself to get you trained to do the same work Helga did for us."

Having made the introduction, Sam left Maya's office. Maya invited Matt to sit down. "Matt, I was a close friend of Helga's, and I too miss her a lot. Whenever she was away from the office the two of us spoke every couple of days by phone. Not all of it was business. She told me about you and how she felt about you. You made her very happy, and she loved you a lot. By her telling me about you I got to like you a lot. And now we meet."

Spontaneously Matt got up and gave Maya a hug. "Thank you. I needed to hear that. I've felt lost ever since I heard I lost her. Can we take a moment to talk about her? I've been longing to speak to someone who knew her. If we talk about her once in a while, you can help me cope."

"That would be good for me too."

From memories about Helga the conversation drifted towards the way Matt felt alienated from his surroundings. Maya sensed his bitterness about losing his support group. "I'm sure you realize that IEDC, like all big companies, is not free from internal rivalries and sometimes there can be disagreements among staff. I want you to know whatever takes place here I'll have your back. The one thing I can still do for Helga is make sure you have a safe place here."

Maya arranged an office for Matt on the fifth floor, right in the center of the technical operations center. Aleksy Dubinski's office was two doors down. Aleksy was head of engineering. He fielded all the calls from the engineers out on location and made sure they got the information they needed. He had solved many problems Helga had had at the Iraqi hydroelectric power plant on the River Zab. Aleksy also knew a lot about Matt and he made it known during their first meeting.

"So, you're Matt. If I had to hear one more word about you I would have screamed." Matt expected the worst, but Aleksy laughed. "Just kidding! It was all good; Helga told me what a wonderful guy you are. She bragged about you. You're a real war hero and I respect that. I date back to Vietnam and have to admit to having been a pussyfoot rifle man. Welcome aboard. I'm glad to have you in my department."

A week after Matt's arrival at IEDC Aleksy gave him a rather simple task. The IEDC crew working in Honduras were getting ready to install a second turbine. Matt's assignment was to order the turbine. He looked up the original order for the first turbine and placed a new order for an additional turbine to be delivered to the IEDC operation working at the newly built dam. The factory had anticipated the need for a second turbine and the unit was ready to be shipped.

Three weeks later IEDC personnel in Honduras started complaining that their work had come to a standstill waiting for the arrival of the additional turbine. Aleksy asked Matt to look into the matter. Matt contacted the factory and was informed that the turbine had been shipped on time and should be in Honduras.

When Matt traced the shipment he discovered the unit was stuck in customs. He learned that when he placed the order for the turbine he should have applied for an import license. The license would have been automatically granted upon presentation of the contract between IEDC and the Honduran government. Since he had failed to get the import license ahead of time, the turbine was stuck in a customs' warehouse. Matt was mortified when he found out it would take at least a week to get the turbine released and shipped on to the small town where the dam had been built.

Rather than go to Aleksy to explain the situation and ask for his help, Matt went straight to Maya's office. He ignored her secretary and burst unannounced into her office. "I quit. I'm leaving. I'm not qualified to work here."

Matt's unannounced entrance surprised Maya but she calmly looked up from the report she was reading. "Hello Matt. I wasn't expecting you. Is everything okay?"

"Thanks for giving me a chance; everybody here is great, but I messed up terribly and have to leave. I'm sorry; I tried but I'm not good enough to work here."

"Did you speak to Aleksy? Does he know you've come to see me?"

"No."

"Then sit down and tell me what is going on." Maya got up from her desk and motioned for Matt to join her on the couch at the side of her desk.

"I forgot to get an import license for the turbine going to Honduras. The damn thing is stuck in customs and it will take at least a week to get it released. Because of my stupidity, IEDC has wasted weeks on the project, and we have to pay storage for the time the turbine is spending in the customs' warehouse."

Maya took Matt's hand and held it for a moment. "Okay, it could have been handled better, but it's not the end of the world. Matt, calm down. Nobody got killed, and I assure you this little mishap won't bankrupt IEDC."

"But you guys trusted me and I screwed up."

"I don't agree. Maybe we screwed up. Someone should have walked you through the process so you would have known to apply for an import license. And you should have felt comfortable enough to ask for more guidance. That said, I don't think something terrible has happened."

"But we're weeks behind schedule on the project."

"Yes, we are. We'll have to straighten that out with the Honduran government. They'll claim damages because of the delay, but that won't happen."

"Are you sure?"

"I'm pretty sure of it. It will be Sam's job to talk them out of making a fuss out of the delay and he's a master at that."

"Won't he be furious at me for causing this mess?"

"I don't think so. You have to understand Sam. He prides himself on his ability to handle situations like this.

He thrives on it, and it helps emphasize his importance to the company."

"He won't think he gave me a chance, and I let him down?"

"Oh, Matt, you make me cry you carry so much hurt. Life has handed you some bad cards. People treated you badly, but life here at IEDC is different. Besides, surely you aren't so egotistical to think you are first one at our company to make a mistake like this? We believe in each other and help each other. Go talk things over with Aleksy. Things will be fine."

Chapter Three

"Where the hell have you been?" Aleksy's greeting when he entered his office caused Matt to doubt Maya's assurance that all would be okay. But Aleksy's warm smile settled him down. "I've been looking all over for you to tell you I settled everything with those bureaucrats in the customs office in Honduras. That turbine is on the way to the dam site and should be there in less than two days."

Matt was stunned. "*You* got the import license?"

"Of course. That's my job. I'm here to support our people on location, and they needed that baby pronto."

"How did you know about my screw up with the import license?"

"Oh, come on. You've been here long enough to know that when our buddies in the field have a problem they come crying to papa Aleksy, also known as Daddy Fixer. As soon as I heard about my screw up, I set out to fix it."

"*Your* screw up?"

"Yeah. I forgot to tell you to get an import license when I told you to order that additional turbine. How the hell were you to know about those cumbersome local restrictions?"

"I could have asked."

"How can you ask about an import license when you've never heard of such a thing? No, it was my bad."

"The point is I know nothing about any of those types of things, and I'm not really qualified to work here."

"You're right. I was born knowing all about import licenses and any other local restrictions. Come on Matt, cut that crap. You're smart enough to learn all this stuff, and from Helga I heard you have something I need in my department."

Matt was curious. "What's that?"

"We work in a lot of countries and deal with many different cultures. Helga said you dealt respectfully with the Kurds. At no time did she feel you felt superior to them just because you were a US officer. What really impressed her was your instinctive ability to recognize the good guys from bad. When working in a foreign country and faced with a different culture, that is the hardest thing for our people to pick up on. That includes me; I'll be relying on you to guide me through tricky situations when we are working outside of the US."

Matt still felt he was getting a free lunch at IEDC because of Helga. "I'm prancing around here under the pretense that I'm one of the engineers, but I never really worked as an engineer. The army let me finish my degree even before they sent me to OCS. That was ages ago. I'm an army officer, not an engineer."

Aleksy took issue with Matt's argument that he was not qualified to work in his department. "So, you're telling me the skills you've learned as a Lieutenant Colonel in the army are not transferrable to your job here?"

"Some of it probably is, but I don't have any engineering experience and this is an engineering department."

"If you're hung up on that we can take care of that."

"What do you mean?"

"The Cockrell School of Engineering is part of the University of Texas right here in Austin. They offer courses which professionals can follow on weekends to get their master's degree in engineering."

"My degree is too stale to be admitted in the master's program. I'd have to start all over and get a whole lot of undergraduate credits before I can qualify for such a program."

Aleksy shook his head. "That's not true. I can get you admitted."

"Sure. You'll just tell them Helga thought I was a good guy, and since she was a topnotch engineer, they'll admit me."

"Don't be foolish. I'm serious. I can get you admitted. Before Sam recruited me for his company I was a full professor at Cockrell School of Engineering. That was a while back, but I'm still head of their committee for academic development, and a close friend of mine teaches a course on engineering management in the graduate division."

Matt had no idea Aleksy was so well connected. "If you can get me in, I'll jump at it, but I'm afraid I won't be able to keep up with other students who recently got their undergraduate degrees in engineering and are working in that field."

Aleksy laughed. "They won't have a private tutor."

Matt did not catch on to what Aleksy was telling him. "Neither will I."

"You'll have one!" Aleksy laughed even louder. "And if I maybe a little boastful, he's pretty good."

Matt was totally confused. "You expect me to hire a tutor? Someone you know."

"You don't have to hire anybody. *I'm* going to be your tutor. You'll follow classes on weekends, and during the week we'll spend a couple evenings going over the material covered during the previous weekend."

"You're willing to spend a couple of evenings a week helping me?"

"That's what I'm offering, yes."

"Why in world would you give up your evenings to help me?"

Aleksy was getting annoyed. "Stop playing *poor me!* You took a couple of hard punches and got knocked down. We know that. But a fighter gets back up, and in your case, the crowd is cheering for you. We're on your side."

"It's hard to believe how things have turned around for me. First there was Jimmy. Then Sam and Maya and now you. No, I can't cry poor me."

"So, you'll go for your masters?"

"I loved studying engineering and never dreamed I would be able to get a masters' degree. If you can get me enrolled, I'd love it!"

"Good, we have a deal. But let me warn you. As an old professor I expect my students to shoot for *magna cum laude.*"

That was the beginning of a close friendship between the two men which would form the basis for Matt's smooth integration into the company.

Chapter Four

Matt had comfortably settled into the IEDC company culture. All was going well . . . until Vanessa reared her pretty head.

Vanessa was Sam's trophy wife. After having been single for quite a few years Sam, much to the disappointment of his only daughter Margie, married Vanessa. Sam doted on his daughter, and she had served as his hostess at all the elaborate social functions his company sponsored. This position now fell to Vanessa. It was an open secret the women hated each other. Margie had been heard referring to Vanessa as that floozy and Vanessa liked calling attention to Margie's bad leg by calling her our cripple.

Matt had met Vanessa during a company dinner in honor of some diplomats from Nigeria who had just signed a contract with IEDC to update several power stations along the Kainji Dam. At the dinner, Vanessa paid a lot of attention to Matt. He thought nothing of it; he figured she was probably just being nice to the new guy.

A week later Vanessa called and invited him to dinner. Again, he thought nothing of it. He had been told Sam often entertained staff at his house which everyone affectionately called the mansion. Matt started worrying when he arrived at the mansion and Vanessa told him Sam was out of town and he was the only guest. He wanted to beg out, but could not think of a way to do that without insulting the boss's wife.

After an elaborate dinner, Vanessa dismissed the servants and asked Matt to join her in the library for an after dinner drink. During the dinner Matt had been careful to limit the amount of wine he drank. When Vanessa opened the well-stocked bar in the library, she asked Matt what he wanted. She was not pleased when he asked for a soft drink. "What's the matter? I noticed you hardly touched your wine during dinner. Are you a teetotaler?" Matt gratefully grabbed on to the excuse. "Yes ma'am, I hardly ever drink alcohol."

"Oh please. Don't ma'am me. Call me Vanessa. Come over here and sit next to me on this nice comfortable couch." Matt went over and sat at the far end of the massive couch.

Vanessa looked at him and patted the space next to her on the coach. When Matt ignored the invitation, she made a gesture as to say have it your way followed by, "All right then. While you sit there and sip your coke I'll go and put on something more comfortable."

When she reappeared, she was wearing a beautiful silk robe which she had not closed all the way in the front. Matt could see that beneath the robe she was only wearing a bra and panties. Her nipples showed through the flimsy material of her bra. With a big smile on her face Vanessa plopped down next to Matt. "So that's better. Now the two of us can get nice and comfy."

Matt stood up. "If you'll excuse me; it's time for me to go home. Thanks for the wonderful dinner, but I've a lot of work to do to prepare for a meeting in the morning."

"Are you queer? Or don't you like what you see?"

By this time Matt was stuttering. He had trouble getting his words out. "No, ma'am . . . Sorry, I mean. No, Vanessa . . . I mean to say . . . No, I'm not queer, and yes, you're beautiful."

"Then what's the matter? Would you rather go into the bedroom? I guess you feel strange fucking me here on the couch in this big library. By the way, don't worry there is nobody else in the house."

By this time Matt had regained a little of his composure. "Vanessa, I think you're beautiful, really I do but I'm still grieving for the woman I lost."

"Yeah I heard about that. But a good roll in the hay will do wonders for you. Come on. I've had the hots for you ever since we met last week at the company dinner."

"Vanessa, please . . . you're my boss's wife."

"So what? I'm asking you to fuck me, not marry me. Here look at this." She pulled open her nightgown and undid her bra. "Here look at these. Have you ever seen tits more beautiful? And these?" She stood up and showed off her legs and began to pull down her panties.

Matt had to admit to himself that she made it tempting, but he turned on his heels and headed for the front door. Vanessa pulled up her panties and followed him. "If you don't come back and satisfy me I'll claim you broke in and tried to rape me. You can't just leave me in this condition; my whole body is aching for yours. Please come with me to the bedroom and make love to me!"

Matt turned around; he was furious and yelled at her. "You tell them whatever you like. I'll go to jail before I cheat on Sam and go to bed with a slut like you."

Chapter Five

Early the next morning Matt came storming into Maya's office. "I can't stay here at IEDC. I have to leave as soon as possible. I'm sorry; all of you have been wonderful, but I must leave."

Maya had no idea what was going on. "Sit down and have a cup of coffee before you tell me why you're breaking my heart."

"Oh, Maya, it's not about you. Far from it. You and all my colleagues have been wonderful. But if I stay, it will cause a lot of trouble and I like all of you too much to disturb things around here."

"Matt, when I told you no matter what I'd have your back, I meant it! Now, out with it. What is going on?"

"It's difficult. I don't what to start trouble for Sam. Not after all he's done for me. That also includes you and Aleksy. All of you have been great. I'm so sorry this had to happen. I swear I didn't do anything wrong."

"So, the problem is Vanessa. What did she do?"

Matt was amazed. "How did you guess?"

"I watched her at the company dinner last week. She wouldn't leave you alone. She devoured you with her eyes like a hungry child devouring a cupcake with extra frosting. Can't say I blame the poor woman. If I may say so you're one hell of a hunk. Like Helga, you're a workout fanatic, and it shows. And that cute face of yours doesn't hurt either. Tell me. What did she do to get you so upset?"

Matt did not respond. His experience in the army was still too fresh for him to accept that someone would automatically be on his side without even knowing all the facts. "Come on, Matt. Tell old Maya what the lady did."

Maya had gotten up from her desk and sat down next to Matt. She leaned over to place her hand on his arm. "Honey, you're not leaving. Now tell me what happened."

Matt took a deep breath. "She tried to get me into bed."

Maya had to hold back a chuckle. "Sorry, I don't mean to laugh about it, but in a very timid way you're telling me she invited you to have sex with her. Right?"

"Yes . . . She tried to seduce me last night."

"Not to be overly nosy, but how did she try that?"

"She invited me to dinner. When I got to the mansion, I found out Sam was away on business and I was the only guest. At that point I tried to beg out, but couldn't think of a way to do it gracefully without hurting her feelings. We had a really fabulous dinner. After we finished dinner, she dismissed the servants. We moved to the library and she literally threw herself at me. When I walked out, she threatened to tell people I came to the mansion and when she invited me in I tried to rape her."

Maya shook her head. "Poor woman. I never thought she'd go to such extremes."

"Why do you say poor woman? She tried to cheat on Sam!"

"Yes, she did. But things aren't exactly what you think. Sam never loved her. When he married her, it was like he had bought another well-known painting for his mansion. She is just another beautiful decoration he brings along when he entertains. He never involves her in any serious discussion; he has no respect for her opinion and often cuts her off when she tries to join a business discussion. True, she isn't the sharpest tack in the box, but she does have feelings. She was a famous super model when they met, and Sam had been a bachelor for a long time. He wanted this beautiful woman to show off on his arm, and she fell in love with the powerful captain of industry."

"I didn't notice any friction at the company dinner."

"Of course not. Sam entertained the guests from Nigeria while Vanessa was left alone to ogle at you."

Matt's dislike for Vanessa started to ease off a little. "I've heard that Sam's daughter and Vanessa don't get along. Whose fault is that?"

"Yes, the two don't like each other. They're both to blame, but it's understandable that they don't get along. Sam loves only two things in this world, his daughter, Margie, and his company. In that order. It's only natural for Vanessa to resent Margie and Margie, who is brilliant, doesn't think Vanessa is worthy of her dad. There you have it, the perfect ingredients for war."

"I haven't met Margie. Where is she?"

"She is in Niger working on the construction of a hydroelectric power plant on the Kandadji. She is in charge of phase two of the project. Like I said, she's one of our most gifted engineers, but Sam is not happy she's so far away from home. He misses her terribly."

"All this is very interesting. I guess Vanessa is not as bad a person as I thought, but that doesn't excuse her actions. How do we get rid of this situation? We can't just forget about it."

"It's time for Sam to get a divorce and send Vanessa on her way."

"How do you envision getting that done?"

"I'll simply tell him to cut the poor girl loose."

"You *what?*"

"Sam's a great visionary, but for practical things he has always relied on me."

"Okay . . . I know you run the daily operations here, but this is a little too personal isn't it?"

"Not really. Sam and I go back a long way. He relies on me for a lot of things. He asks me what to wear when he's not sure if an occasion is formal or not. Hell, I even go to the mansion and help pack his suitcase when his so-called butler is not available. He'd forget half the stuff he needs if left to pack by himself."

Matt was hesitant to ask what he was thinking but finally said, "Maybe I'm out of line to ask, but what about you and Sam?"

"Like I said we go way back. I came in as a management trainee. Sam singled me out and became my mentor. He sent me to GSEM in Geneva, Switzerland, to get a degree in economics and business management. He paid for the whole thing. That showed he really cared for me. But, if you are asking about anything beyond that, anything more was never likely to develop. Be realistic, I'm a tall skinny broad, and I have never heard anyone say I was good looking. As good friends, Sam and I can spend a long night drinking and playing poker and sex would never even enter Sam's mind."

"What about you? It sounds like you more than just like him."

"Hey, sonny, let's not go there!"

"Got it! I'll mind my own business. But I'll love you forever for getting me out of this mess with Vanessa. Seriously Maya, from the moment I arrived here, you've been like a mom looking out for me. I don't know what I've done to deserve this, but I want you to know I appreciate it."

"Matt, guess what? I like you."

Chapter Six

It took no more than a long talk with Sam for him to agree to divorce Vanessa. Persuading Vanessa to agree was difficult. Maya had to call in the help of Piet Bailey a wildcatter who drilled for oil all over the country. Piet was a regular at Sam's extravagant parties and Maya had often watched him drool over Vanessa. He was obviously crazy about her. Maya just had to signal him that the coast was clear, and he went after her. Sam and Vanessa had a pre-nup, but Vanessa was so infatuated with Sam during their courtship that she demanded little or no input in the drafting of the document. The agreement called for her to get a relatively small sum. To clear his conscience, Sam threw a couple extra million into the final settlement.

All this took place out of Matt's sight. He knew the incident with Vanessa would have no further consequences for him. And several months later, Vanessa was gone. Meanwhile his career at IEDC was taking off. Aleksy assigned him to the team selected to go to Bolivia. There had been an explosion in one of the power plants threatening the collapse of a large dam. The Bolivian government had asked IEDC to assist. The selection of members for the emergency relief team had been unusually competitive; Matt's selection was a tribute to the progress he made since his arrival.

While he was in Bolivia, Matt heard that Margie was home visiting with her father. He was sorry to learn when he got back in Austin that she had already returned to Niger. He had hoped to meet her.

Several months after Matt returned from Bolivia all hell broke out in IEDC. A group of armed rebels had attacked the construction site at the Kandadji dam, killing several security guards. The company first heard what had happened through a call from a reporter at Reuters International. Margie was kidnapped! The news that Margie had been kidnapped by a rebel group in Niger hit IEDC like a bomb. That's all the reporter knew. As the news spread through the company, everybody panicked. What was happening to Margie? Sam appeared to be going crazy. Maya grabbed the phone and called her government contacts in Niamey, the capital city of Niger. They had not been informed of the raid, but promised to contact the army and report back. It took several hours before Maya heard back. The army had started a nationwide search. The rebels had been identified as a breakaway group from the army of a warlord who had been very active during the tension between foreign oil companies and local minorities in the oil-rich delta region.

Sam decided to personally go to Niger to get his daughter back. He had been to Niger several times before to negotiate contracts, and he was sure he could call on his contacts to beef up the search for Margie. His visa was renewed in less than two days. Sam left for Niamey three days after his daughter had been grabbed from the construction site.

Against the wishes of the US government and the government of Niger, Sam announced he was willing to pay a ransom of five million dollars in exchange for the unharmed release of his daughter. A week went by without a nibble, and Sam added a one million reward for any information as to Margie's whereabouts. The army commander charged with the search for Margie complained that Sam was interfering with the search. The government politely, but firmly, asked Sam to leave the country.

Upon his return to the US, Sam kept working behind the scenes. He thought he had hit pay dirt when a demand for one million dollars in gold arrived. The exchange was to be made in the small neighboring country of Burkina Faso. The proof supplied that Margie was alive and under their control was flimsy. Sam was advised not to respond, but he was desperate. He ordered a million dollars in gold to be prepared for shipment and dispatched an armed crew to make the exchange.

When they arrived in Burkina Faso the crew carrying the gold was persuaded to across the border into Benin. In Benin they ran into an ambush. They lost their weapons and the gold. They did not have a clue who their attackers were. The failed attempt to get his daughter back didn't stop Sam. He decided that if the Niger army couldn't locate Margie, he would send his own army to find her. He started to recruit a group of mercenaries which he wanted to arm and send to Niger.

Matt heard about Sam's ill-conceived plan and went to speak to Maya. "Maya, you have to stop him. It's stupid what he's doing. If she is still alive at this late date, he'll get her killed by sending a bunch of bozos to find her."

"Yes. It's a ridiculous idea, but I can't talk him out of it. He's obsessed; he has to get his daughter back, and he'll try anything."

"Let me talk to him."

"Honey, I know you care, but what in the world can you say that I and others haven't already? He won't listen to anyone. He's adamant; he plans to send his own army to get her."

"Maya I need you to tell him to sit down and listen to me. I know he'll do that if you push him hard enough."

"I'll try. For Margie's sake, I hope you can get through to him. Do you have an alternate plan?"

"Never mind what I want to do; just get me in front of him."

As she had done most evenings during the crisis, Maya drove Sam home and stayed with him for dinner at the mansion. When Sam mentioned that he had not yet found anyone suited to lead his army, Maya brought up Matt's request. "He just wants to talk to you."

"What the hell can he do that I haven't tried?"

"Sam, don't be stubborn. Matt has a good head on his shoulders. He's gone through one hell of a bad experience and come through okay. Besides our Helga told us he's very special; just listen to what he has to say."

Though it seemed Sam was not taking advice from anyone during the crisis, he still relied heavily on Maya. "Okay, call him. It's still early. Have him come over and tell us what he can do."

When Matt got the call, he jumped in his car and raced over to the mansion. Sam and Maya were waiting for him in the library. When he entered the library, Matt thought back for a moment to the night Vanessa had tried to lure him into having sex with her. Thank goodness he hadn't given in to her tempting advances. He turned down the drink Maya offered him and got right to the point.

"Sam, please don't send a group of unqualified mercenaries. They'll do more harm than good."

Sam interrupted him with an angry outburst. "You want me to just sit back and do nothing? Just forget about my child being held by a bunch of rebels? Never! Do you hear me, *never*."

"I would never suggest that. Send me. I'll bring your daughter back."

For a moment Sam was speechless. Was Matt serious? "Are you kidding? Send you? All by yourself to get Margie?"

"Nothing has worked for you so far. So, it's up to me to get her back."

Maya was as surprised as Sam. "Matt, are you telling us you can locate Margie and bring her back. All by yourself?"

Sam was skeptical. "I'm desperate enough to send you if I thought you could do it. But all by yourself? How could you possibly do what the whole Niger army can't?"

"I'm a trained army officer. I've fought against insurgents; I can handle a bunch of footloose rebels."

"That doesn't mean you can do what the army has thus far failed to do."

"The difference between me and those men in the army is called determination. Sam, you gave me back my life by allowing me to come and work here. I owe you big time. I'll bring your daughter home."

Chapter Seven

Preparations for Matt's trip to Niger required getting a new visa and the necessary vaccinations. A letter of introduction stated that he was sent by IEDC to work on the project Margie had been working on. Upon his arrival in Niger, Matt checked in with the crew working on the Kandadji power plant. He did not stay there very long. Before leaving the US, he had inquired about a small detachment of US troops stationed in Niger. He contacted them and asked permission to meet with their commander.

He met Captain Conroy in a small restaurant in Agadez. In order not to call attention to their meeting, the captain was dressed in civilian clothes. Matt explained his mission to Captain Conroy. The captain had heard about Margie being kidnapped, but because of the covert mission of their unit they were instructed not to openly intervene.

Matt assured Captain Conroy that he would be careful not to compromise his mission. However, he did need help in securing several items he would need to cover his plan to pose as a secret trophy hunter. It was impossible to bring these items openly into the country. He wanted Captain Conroy to bring them in as military supplies. Military shipments were barely, if ever, checked. The captain agreed in principle, but before giving his final okay he wanted a complete list of the items.

Matt had prepared the list ahead of time. "Fair enough, I have my list ready. I'll read it to you so you can ask about items you're not familiar with. Because I'll pretend to be after African elephants and lions, I'll need pretty heavy duty gear to make it believable. To start with, that includes a powerful tranquillizer gun. Next, I'll need tranquilizer darts carrying a syringe with a strong barbiturate to induce an almost instant coma. The syringes will have to have collared needles. Only an amateur would use straight needles that fall out when the animal shakes after being hit. I'll let the guide kill the animal, so I don't have to carry a regular rifle. I will need a pair of infrared binoculars in case we track the animals by night and a large water canteen I can hang on my belt in case we track on a hot day. IEDC has a copy of this list and will purchase the equipment for me, except for the binoculars which are army issue and can't be purchased on the open market. My company will ship the equipment to a place designated by you. The shipment will be labeled military equipment."

Captain Conroy was impressed. "Sounds like you thought this whole thing through pretty well. Don't worry about the binoculars I have several sets. We use them all the time. How did you know about military issue infrared binoculars?"

"I'm a retired Lieutenant Colonel."

"Welcome to Niger, colonel. No wonder you knew about my unit stationed here in Niger. With your permission, I'll discus your plan with my contact in the Niger military. He's pretty high up on the totem pole. I'm sure he can arrange that at the same time the police don't arrest you while you're posing as a trophy hunter."

"That would be great. Thank you." Matt had told Captain Conroy only half the story. True, he did intend to pose as a trophy hunter in order to try to learn where

Margie was being held. He did not reveal his intention to personally move in and free Margie from her captors rather than give her location to the Niger Army and let them free her. He was afraid that if the army raided the rebel hideout Margie would get killed in the chaos. Having never operated alongside the Niger Army, he had no idea of their efficiency. He did not dare risk an unsuccessful raid. He figured the tranquilizer gun would be useful in the event he had to immobilize several guards.

Chapter Eight

While he was working as an IEDC engineer on the power station, Matt carefully spread the word that he was looking for a guide to take him trophy hunting. Trophy hunting is illegal in Niger, so Matt offered a nice sum of money for a guide. An array of men showed up applying for the job. They all claimed to have wide experience, but Matt turned them all down. He was looking for a specific type. He wanted a person who had been a member of the NDPVF, led by Asani Dokubo in their fight against the government.

Finally, a man named Dimiem approached him. Matt was having a drink with several colleagues from work in a down and dirty bar near the power station when Dimiem pulled him away from the group. "I can show you the best places. But I'll need more money than you're offering. The area where I'll take you is heavily patrolled, but I know the inspector in one section. He patrols the best area."

"I'll pay more, but why should I trust you? You could be a government inspector."

Dimiem laughed. "Me a government inspector? That's a joke."

Matt started to suspect he might have the right man. "Why is that a joke?"

"This government doesn't like members of the NDPVF. Even if you left the movement a long time ago, they still won't hire you."

"I think I can use you. Come with me to the table in the back. I have a lucrative job for you, but it's very private. I don't want the others to hear me."

They sat down at an isolated table at the back of the bar. Dimiem was curious. "So, what is this big deal you can offer me?"

"Have you heard that a young woman was kidnapped from the IEDC work site at the dam?"

"No. I don't know what you're talking about."

Matt laughed. "Okay, have it your way. But that means I can't use you."

Dimiem quickly corrected himself. "Yes, I've heard."

"I thought so. As an ex NDPVF soldier you must know all about the small breakaway groups that are still active. What I need from you is information about the location where this woman is being held."

"Are you crazy? You want to get me killed?"

"I think you're too smart for that. You're well-connected and can find out where she is kept. I'll pay you big money for the information."

"What is big?"

"Ten thousand dollars in cash."

That got Dimiem's attention. "I get two thousand for leading a hunt. That can put me in jail if they catch me. This could get me killed. How about fifty thousand?"

"I can get someone else to give me the information. Do you want to work with me or not?"

"Okay, already! I'm just trying. Can you offer a little more?"

Matt was sure Dimiem would do it for ten thousand. "No!"

"How long do I have?"

"As fast as you can get the information."

"When do I get the money? Can you give me some now?"

"Dimiem, I have to trust you. You could lead me into a trap. I'll have to trust you, and you'll have to trust me if we're going to work together. I'll give you the full amount when we meet and you tell me her location."

Dimiem agreed. "I'll contact you when I have some information. By the way the rebels don't want money. They want weapons, and the government doesn't want to deal with them."

"Is she still alive?"

"As far as I know, yes. But not for much longer. If the government continues to refuse to deal with them, they'll kill her and move on."

"That makes it urgent. Get me her location!"

Dimiem left and Matt stepped outside to call Maya. It was well past seven in the evening and because of the six-hour time difference Matt knew Maya might not answer. A sleepy voice answered.

"Maya it's me Matt." In an instant Maya was wide awake.

"Matt…is she alive?"

"Yes, and I'm finally on track to find her. I need cash to pay an informer."

"How much and when?"

"Send ten thousand in cash by courier. If you can arrange it do it tomorrow. Anyway, no later than by the end of the week."

"Will do. Matt are you okay? Now we're also worried about you."

"Don't worry; I'm okay. Tell Sam I'll bring Margie home. From now on, if I need you, I'll call Aleksy's phone. It's known I call him about work, and you never know who's watching."

Chapter Nine

Matt checked the big company SUV out of the motor pool and headed to a town called Zinder where he had arranged to meet Dimiem. The tranquillizer gun and all the other equipment he had asked Captain Conway for was packed safely in the back. A non-descript old briefcase packed with hundred dollar bills was lying on the floor in front of the passenger seat.

Dimiem had called to tell him he knew the exact location where Margie was being held. Matt did not want to waste any time; he was ready to go after her. They met at the Gamzaki De Zinder Hotel in Zinder. Dimiem was waiting for him when Matt entered the hotel lobby. They didn't waste any time on small talk. Matt asked, "Do you have a map or something to show me."

"Yeah, but it's not that simple. She's in Chad."

"She's what!? They took her out of Niger?"

"Yes, they are holding her not far across the border in a remote area. I've hunted there."

"Damn it! I'll need a visa to get into Chad."

"You know nothing about this area of the world. The moment you cross the border, they'll know about it."

"Then what can I do?"

"I'll take you across the border. We'll follow the route I use while hunting with my clients. In that remote area, there are few patrols. If they catch us they know I'll give them a percentage of the fee the hunters pay me."

"Do we go across the border by foot?"

"Don't be stupid. You can't walk all the way to their location. They operate out of a big compound that used to belong to a murdered warlord. It's about fifty miles from the border. I'll take you halfway there. You'll follow me in my truck."

It took two days to reach the stretch of the border where Dimiem knew it was safe to cross. If he had not seen the remnants of a fence that had collapsed a long time ago, Matt would not even have known they had crossed into Chad. The road was practically nonexistent. Matt's late model SUV could easily keep up with Dimiem's dilapidated old pickup, but Matt was less adept at negotiating the sharp bends and deep ruts than Dimiem; he barely kept up.

When they approached a remote village, Dimiem stopped and walked over to Matt's SUV. "Okay, this is as far as I go. Get out we have to switch vehicles."

"What do you mean by switch vehicles?"

"In this area, when they see that nice shiny SUV you won't be long for this world. From here on out you'll drive my truck. I'll take the SUV back. Ten thousand for locating your friend. The SUV for taking you across the border."

Matt wanted to protest but realized he had no choice. The SUV would stick out like a sore thumb, and he could not park it there until he returned. Besides Dimiem had to have a way to get back to Niger. "Okay, but I have to transfer my equipment first."

"Don't forget to give me the money."

"You haven't shown me where that compound is."

Dimiem pulled out a map and showed Matt how to get to the compound where Margie was kept. He pointed to the road which led to the front of the compound and warned Matt not to take it. Pointing to an area he had marked on the map, he said, "This area is heavily wooded. If you leave the truck there you can follow the path I have highlighted on foot. It leads to the back of the compound. The compound is protected by a fence, but there is a gate at the end of the path. I have to warn you. Like the main gate in the front, it is always guarded. Sometimes even by two men."

"Thanks for the warning. I'll be careful."

"Going there by yourself is not what I call careful. Just in case you happen to survive this crazy mission, I recommend that you backtrack all the way across the border to Niger and seek shelter in the nearest army base. I have marked one on the map which is less than fifty miles from the border."

Matt handed Dimiem the briefcase and shook his hand. "You have more than earned the money and the SUV."

Dimiem had one more thing. He went over to the SUV removed the private vehicle license plate and replaced it with a green international organization plate. "So, now I can safely drive around in this beautiful car." Next, he removed the plate from his truck and screwed the one from the SUV in its place. "If you get caught, I don't want to be a dead duck when they trace my plate. By the way, there is a large camouflage tarp in the back of my truck. Cover the truck when you park it in the woods." He got into the SUV and drove off.

Matt got into Dimiem's truck and headed in the direction of the village. He was happy no one took notice of his passing through. He had no trouble finding the road which led to the woods Dimiem had marked on his map. The road was horrible, and it took much longer than he expected to get there.

Once he got into the woods he found a snug place between two trees where he could park the truck and keep it as much as possible out of sight. For extra security, he threw the tarp over the truck. He sat in the truck waiting for dusk. To keep his nerves under control he focused his mind on only one thing, *I have to get Margie out of that compound without alerting the rebels. I may have to kill to do it. This is war and I'm trained to carry out my mission.*

When it was dark enough to venture onto the footpath, he took the tranquillizer gun and the other equipment and headed for the compound. He knew from the map that the path was over two miles long but he walked so fast that it surprised him when the gate loomed up out of the darkness. Quickly he hit the dirt hoping the guards had not seen him. A small branch cracked under his weight. The guards heard it. They both lowered their rifles and one of them carefully started walking down the path. He pointed his rifle into the darkness and came within fifty feet of where Matt was crouched down. Matt cursed himself for his stupid mistake. *I came so close and now I fucked up. I wish I had loaded a dart. That would have given me a chance; I could have taken him down and gone after the other guard after re-loading.*

Matt lay perfectly still for several minutes, barely breathing for fear the guard would hear him. The guard used his rifle to poke around the bushes. When he was within twenty feet Matt prepared to jump him. To his relief the guard turned around and yelled something to the other guard. Matt could not understand what he was saying. The guard shouldered his rifle and returned to the gate. When he was absolutely sure he had not been noticed, Matt retreated several hundred feet and climbed onto a small mound. Through his night vision binoculars, he studied the gate. Beyond the gate he could see the outline of a big house and to the left of the big house he could see a much smaller building. Matt wondered where they kept Margie. According to Dimiem the group holding her might be as big as thirty men.

After Matt had been studying the compound for a while he saw a man emerge from the main building carrying what looked like a plate of food. The man proceeded to the smaller building and entered. After a while he emerged without the plate and returned to the main building. Matt was sure this indicated Margie was in the smaller building and the man had just brought her some food. Since no one came to the door to open it, Matt concluded there were no guards inside. That meant Margie was alone in the building. Once again, Matt focused his binoculars on the guards. He did not have an infrared scope on the tranquilizer gun so he could not take a shot at them in the dark. He had to wait for sunrise. In the meantime, he timed the interval between the changes of the guards.

When he had sufficient sunlight, Matt settled into a comfortable prone position and readied the tranquilizer gun for a shot. He had timed the interval between the changing of the guards. It was three hours, and two new guards had just arrived. He had plenty of time to make it to the smaller building.

He aimed very carefully at one of the guards leaning against the fence. He placed the cross hairs of his scope on the man's neck and slowly pulled the trigger. The tranquillizer gun barely made a sound. The guard grabbed for his throat, staggered and fell to the ground. The other guard raced over to see what was happening. Matt had already loaded another dart and he hit the second guard right between the shoulders. Matt dropped the gun and ran for the gate. The guards were sprawled on the ground; he ran past them heading straight for the small building.

As he burst through the unlocked door he saw a woman dressed in fatigues, much the same as Helga had worn, lying on a make shift cot. He assumed it was Margie. His sudden appearance frightened her; she pulled back when he approached her. "Come on let's get out of here!" Matt yelled.

The woman pulled away even further. "Who are you? What do you want?"

"Your father sent me to bring you home. Come on let's go!"

"I can't. They took my brace. I can't walk."

Matt could not waste any time. "I'll carry you."

Before Matt could lift her Margie yelled. "Watch out! Behind you!"

Matt turned just in time to see two men coming at him. They must have seen him from the big house and followed him. One of the men was holding a knife. In an instant Matt's army training set in. He lunged at the man brandishing the knife and took him down while snatching the knife away. The other man jumped on top of them and tried to pry the knife from Matt's firm grip. The three of them were rolling on the ground. Matt pulled his arm free and plunged the knife into the heart of one of his attackers. He grabbed the other man by the throat and squeezed with both hands. The man's eyes bulged as he tried to breathe, but Matt held on until the man was dead.

Margie watched the whole thing in horror. Matt swooped her up in his arms and said, "Hold on, we're going home." He raced to the gate, passed the two unconscious guards and ran all the way down the path carrying Margie in his arms. She had her arms around his neck and held on so tight that he had to ask her to give him some room to breathe. Matt didn't stop running until they reached the pickup.

Still holding Margie in his arms, he ripped of the tarp. Next, he got her into the passenger seat and quickly ran around to get into the driver's seat. As he started the engine he yelled, "Hold on! This might be a bumpy ride, but we're going home."

Chapter Ten

The trip back to the border went without incident but once they crossed into Niger, Matt had trouble finding the army base. By this time Margie had recovered from the shock of her violent rescue and had regained enough of her composure to ask, "Who are you? How were you able to run all the way down that pass?"

"I'm Matt. We've never met, but I work for your dad at IEDC. I promised him I'd bring you home, and we had to get out of there in a hurry before they caught up to us. By the way, are you ready to speak to your dad?"

"I'm still a little shaky. But, yes. I want to talk to my dad."

Matt stopped on the side of the road and called Sam. Maya answered Sam's phone. "Maya, this is Matt, let me speak to Sam."

"Matt! Is everything okay? Are you safe?"

"All okay. Put Sam on."

Matt handed the phone to Margie. "Daddy, it's me Margie."

Matt could not hear Sam's response, but it brought Margie to tears.

"Really, Daddy, I'm okay! This superman came to get me. Daddy I'm free!"

After Margie and her dad spoke for a while, Margie handed the phone to Matt. "Here, Dad wants to speak to you."

Sam could hardly speak he was so emotional. "Thank you, thank you, thank you. You brought my baby back. God bless you Matt. You're the greatest man alive. You did it! You found her!"

Matt interrupted Sam. "Sam, I feel so lucky that I was able to do this. I had to do it for you, Maya and for myself."

Sam wanted to know how the rescue went. "Not now, Sam. There will be plenty of time when we get back. Now I have to get us safely to a Niger army base. Can you or Maya call your contacts in the Niger government or military? Please tell them that according to my map we'll be arriving at army barracks twenty-two fairly soon. We'll need permission to enter the post."

They arrived less than an hour later. The post commander was at the gate to greet them. After suffering through a hero's welcome, Matt asked the commander if he could arrange a helicopter to fly Margie to the hospital in Niamey for a complete checkup before she returned to the US. The commander was happy to make all arrangements. He also wanted to know how and where Matt found Margie. He confessed that his men had searched for months without success. Matt did not want to disclose that he knew that the rebels wanted weapons and that the Niger government had been negotiating all along with them. Matt did not tell the commander that Margie had been kept in Chad. He was very vague and promised to file a complete report later.

Margie refused to board the helicopter by herself. She had been clinging to Matt since their arrival on post. She had been given a set of crutches and could have managed to board by herself but she was still scared and needed to hold onto Matt for security. Matt assured her he would be at her side until they arrived home in Austin.

At the hospital the doctors determined that Margie was basically in good health. She had lost a lot of weight due to the poor diet her captors had kept her on, and she was weak due to her prolonged inactively. The hospital did not have the correct brace to fit her leg so they gave her a better set of crutches and encouraged her to start walking as much as possible.

After Matt made sure Margie was in good health and could safely make the long trip home, he called Maya to book their flight. Margie slept like a log on the plane. She was embarrassed when she woke up to find out she'd spent most of the flight snuggled against Matt's chest. When she apologized, Matt quipped, "I think the guy across the aisle from us was jealous."

The arrival in Austin was chaotic. Over half the employees of IEDC had come to the airport. Besides the IEDC people, the arrival hall was filled with members of the local and national press. Several TV stations had set up cameras to capture Margie's reunion with her dad. Matt had been warned by the cabin crew what to expect. As soon as he slid Margie into the arms of her father, he tried to escape the crowd with the help of one of the stewardesses. He did not get very far before Maya caught up to him. She quickly guided him to a waiting limo.

Inside the car she hugged and kissed him. "Matt, we love you so much. You brought our Margie home. You're our hero; Sam said the company is yours. We can't possibly repay you for bringing his baby home. I dreamt and prayed you could do it, *and you did it.* Here let me give you another hug."

All Matt wanted was to get to his apartment away from the crowd. He told Maya he was bushed from the long trip and needed to lie down for a while.

Back at his apartment, he poured himself a stiff drink, pulled the curtains closed and lay down fully dressed on his bed. From the moment he arrived in Niger he had felt tense, wound up like a tight spring. Finally, he could feel his body relax; the spring was slowly unwinding. Over and over again, people had called him a hero. He didn't feel like a hero. Why did he risk his life to rescue Margie? Did he risk her life? The answer to the last question came easy. No. Dimiem had made it very clear; she would be killed if she was not rescued. But why did he feel so strongly that it was up to him to rescue her?

He had felt the same way when in Afghanistan he jumped out of the helicopter to rescue the crew from the burning helicopter. He had to. Helicopter crews had repeatedly come to the rescue when his unit was pinned down by the enemy. He owed them. This time, he had owed Sam.

The next day Matt could not escape the hero's welcome he received when he returned to the office. From the moment he entered the building, people ran up to him to thank him. The men shook his hand till he thought it would fall off and the women showered him with kisses. He could hardly enter his office. It was filled wall to wall with beautiful bouquets of flowers.

Aleksy had tears in his eyes when he embraced him. "I told you, you had a special talent, and we would need you to deal with difficult situations in foreign countries. But this goes beyond everything. Matt you're very special person, and I'm proud to be your friend. Come with me. We have a date with Sam."

The two of them drove to the Ferrari dealer. Sam met them in the showroom. He greeted Matt with, "I love you like a son, but I hate that old clunker you drive around in. I want my heroes to drive around in respectable cars. Look around the show room - what color do you like?"

Matt knew Sam was grateful, but he had not expected anything like this. "Sam, I appreciate the gesture, but really you don't have to do this. Really, this is too much. What I did was my duty. As a trained army officer, I was the one to get Margie. The army trained me to deal with insurgents. It was my privilege to bring her home."

Sam would have nothing of Matt's protestations. "Okay, Okay. I hear you but I'm a stubborn old man, and the hero who rescued my Margie can't ride around in an old clunker. Now, go ahead and select one of these cars."

Matt circled around the showroom. All the cars were gorgeous, and it was difficult to make a choice. Finally, Matt choose a blue Portofino. Sam had been watching and had seen that Matt had carefully checked the price tag of each model and the Portofino was the cheapest.

Carefully Sam tried to steer Matt away from the cheapest model. "Your present car is an old station wagon. The Portofino is a sleek car, but it's a two seater. Do you think you'll be happy with that? Take a look at the GTC4LUSSO over there. It's a sports car and station wagon rolled into one, Besides, it's really beautiful."

Matt hesitated, and Sam to see he would clearly prefer that car. Sam laughed, "I know it's more than 100K more, but I would love for you to have it. Go ahead. Tell the salesman what color you want."

Chapter Eleven

It took a while for things to get back to normal at IEDC. Sam stopped hovering over Margie and once again fully immersed himself in the problems of the company. Maya stopped encouraging Margie to eat more in order to gain back her weight. She didn't nag. She did it by repeatedly inviting Margie to an elaborate home cooked meal. Sam and Matt were also invited to these dinners, and the four of them spent quite a few evenings together at Maya's house.

Matt loved those evenings, but he was afraid it could spoil his relationships with his colleagues, especially with his direct boss Aleksy. It might look like he was exploiting Sam's gratitude. He spoke to Maya about it. Maya understood but told him Margie would object if she didn't invite him. Matt didn't catch on right away. "Look, I understand she's grateful I came to get her in Chad, but that does not mean I have to be invited to every dinner with you three."

"Matt, I'm sure she's grateful, but she wants me to invite you because she likes you. Haven't you noticed how frequently she drops by your office to chat?"

Matt was surprised. "Do you two talk about me? Do you two discuss her boyfriends?"

"Yes, we've talked about you. And no, she has no boyfriends. Let me tell you more about Margie and you'll understand why there are no boyfriends. She's afraid her wounds will scare them away. Margie was fourteen when she and her mom got into a serious car accident. Her mom was killed and Margie was seriously wounded. I spent weeks at the hospital trying to comfort her. The doctors saved her mangled right leg, but she lost the use of it. She can't stand on it; that's why she has that heavy brace. The rest of her body was pretty mangled, too. The doctors managed to repair her damaged organs but despite endless skin grafts, her back is still a mess. She is very self-conscious of her leg and her back. She always wears slacks. Except for me, she allows no one to see her bare back or leg. Not even her dad."

Matt knew about the bad leg but this was the first he had heard about the accident and Margie's back. "Wow, poor kid. And that must have been hard on Sam. Losing his wife and having his child badly wounded."

"Yes, the whole affair was tragic. It was a one car accident. Sam's wife was at the wheel; she was drunk. She was an alcoholic. We all felt we should have done more to help her stop drinking. To this day, Sam still carries some of that guilt. His total obsession with growing the company did not help erase the hurt or the feeling that his neglect was partly to blame for his wife's alcohol problem. In his defense, I have to say she was very clever at hiding her drinking. Margie, on the other hand, carries a grudge. She'll never forgive her mother for causing the accident that maimed her."

"I didn't have a clue. I've seen her with lots of her girlfriends. Never noticed there were no boys around."

Maya shook her head. "Yes, it's a shame. She's not beautiful like her mother was, but she is kind of cute. She's convinced men will find her scars so gross that she holds them at arm's length. I've tried to reason with her, but to no avail. Matt, she likes you a lot. Please be nice to her, be her friend. That's all she asks, and you would do me a great favor."

"Of course, I'll be her friend. She's brilliant, and I find her a nice person to be with. I really enjoy her company."

Maya smiled at him. "There is a reason I like you so much. Besides being incredibly brave, you're a nice man."

Matt had no trouble being nice to Margie. She never acted like the boss's daughter or threw around her great wealth. Her sports car was the envy of most of her friends, but she never insisted on driving herself and was happy to go places with Matt. When they went places with a group of friends, she discretely paid for herself when appropriate, but never embarrassed Matt by picking up the tab when he was given the bill.

A problem arose when an old hydroelectric power plant in Egypt needed repair. IEDC got the contract to repair the power plant. Margie was the ideal person to head the team going to Egypt to work on the power plant because she was one of the top engineers in the company. But after her experience in Niger, she was afraid to travel abroad. Even if she had wanted to go, Sam would not have allowed it. Matt was ready to volunteer, but Aleksy politely informed him that he was not qualified to head the project.

Two months later an identical problem arose. One of the three units at the Betania hydroelectric power plant in Columbia had stopped functioning. The company that had built it back in nineteen eighty-seven requested assistance, and IEDC was hired to help make repairs. All senior engineers were out on location working on projects from which they could not be diverted. Besides Aleksy, Margie was the only engineer left who could handle the project. For Aleksy to go would seriously disrupt communications with the service teams on location therefore Margie decided she had to go.

Matt was reviewing progress reports sent in by the team in Egypt when Margie came into his office. "Mind if I sit down? I have something I have to ask you."

Matt was happy to see her. "Please, sit down. Can I get you a coffee or something?"

"No. I'm good, thanks. I want to talk to you about the project in Columbia."

"Yeah, when it rains it pours. We have too many projects going on. Aleksy himself might go, and I'll be panic-stricken having to take his place here."

"Don't worry. *I'm* planning on going."

"Really? I'm surprised. I thought you weren't ready to travel yet."

"I'll go, but only if you agree to come with me. I'm still scared, but I'll feel safe if you come along."

"Come on, we can't redo Chad."

"Matt, I'm serious! Don't make fun of me. I'll feel safe if you're with me."

"That's one hell of a compliment. Have you discussed this with Aleksy?'

"He agrees, but only if Dad okays it."

"He'll never agree. He won't let you go to Columbia. Are you kidding? Columbia of all places. He'll never allow you to go. That plant in Betania is a stone's throw from Medellin. Sam will throw a fit."

"You might be wrong. He thinks you can walk on water, and I think he'll leave it up to me. I'll go straight up to his office to ask."

Chapter Twelve

The IEDC crew flew by chartered plane to Columbia. During the flight, the ones who had been on assignment abroad before briefed their new colleagues on what to expect. Egged on by Margie, they related some of their funnier experiences. Margie's kidnapping was not mentioned, but it was alluded to when someone teased her that she was bringing her security blanket along. Margie laughed and coyly replied, "Maybe it's just to keep me warm." Matt could feel his ears turn red.

Upon landing, the plane was met by a patrol of the Columbian army. Frightened, Margie called Maya. "The army has surrounded our plane; don't they expect us?"

"Don't worry honey. Your father arranged it. He insisted on military protection for our crew before he agreed to let you leave for Columbia."

"Why didn't you tell me?"

"He thought you and the rest of the crew would object. Besides, he didn't figure on such an obvious show of force. He thought the government would make a more subtle arrangement."

Margie laughed. "Well let me tell you, this ain't subtle. The only thing they left out is a set of tanks."

"Better safe than sorry."

"Okay, we'll live with it."

Margie went out on the tarmac to meet Lieutenant Alfredo, a pleasant looking young man in his late twenties. Lieutenant Alfredo shook her hand and offered a gracious welcome, "Welcome to Columbia. My unit will be with you during your stay here in my country. Your company asked for military protection. They think the drug dealers will harm you. Please don't believe everything they say about us in your country. We're a friendly country and love to have visitors. Medellin is falsely painted as a dangerous place. I was born and raised here and have never had any trouble. Besides, Pablo Escobar is dead and we're trying to become a tourist destination. If your work at the power plant allows it, I would love to show you around my city."

A large tour bus was waiting to take the IEDC crew to Betania. Alfredo's platoon escorted the bus along the route. The road was in such horrible condition that it took almost three hours to go from Medellin airport to Betania. The National University of Columbia had used the local office of the Regional Forestry Reserve to find accommodations for the crew. The rooms they found were clean, but far from luxurious. Nobody complained. They were not on vacation; they were there to work. As Margie told them, "We're here to get the job done and return home as soon as possible." She led by example, but took enough time out to teach Matt the intricacies of machinery he had never worked on before. He caught on quickly, partly due to his native talent, but it helped that she was the most thorough and patient instructor he had ever had.

After two weeks the work was almost done and Margie and Matt decided take Alfredo up on his offer to show them around Medellin.

Alfredo was delighted, but balked on the idea of a one day trip. "Just going back and forth will take a day. To give you some idea what Medellin is like, I need at least two days. They agreed, and he booked two rooms in Hotel Estelar Blue for two nights.

Alfredo's tour of Medellin started in Pueblito Pasia, a traditional Colombian village within the city. He gave them a detailed tour of the village after which he suggested they take some time to shop for souvenirs in the street markets. They did not buy anything, but Margie loved it and she dragged Matt by the arm into small shops to critically examine work by local artists. Margie's lame leg made walking long distances difficult, so she used Matt's arm for support as she enthusiastically followed Alfredo to a market where they sampled local snacks.

After they visited a site to view a panoramic view of the Medellin Valley, they travelled downtown for what Alfredo called a dose of urban culture. They toured the Zen-inspired Barefoot Park, the Park of Lights, and Fernando Botero Plaza with its twenty-three giant bronze statues.

For dinner Alfredo suggested Hacienda-Junim known for its excellent local cuisine. By the time they finished dinner, they were exhausted and it was time to check in at their hotel. Alfredo and two of his men checked the lobby and walked them to the elevator. Even though he knew the hotel was safe, Matt walked Margie to her room.

When she unlocked her door Matt hesitated. He wanted to kiss her goodnight, but thought that would be inappropriate, so he just said, "What time do you want to meet downstairs for breakfast?"

Margie was all smiles. "Today was so nice, I loved every minute of it, but I'm bushed and need some sleep.

How about eight? Is that okay for you?" Matt agreed and went down the hall to his room.

The next morning they were still having breakfast when Alfredo arrived. He had already eaten but was happy to join them for coffee. Over coffee he explained, "First, I want to take you on the aerial metro cable. We'll soar over the city to the top of a mountain where we'll explore a hilltop commune. After that, we'll leave the city and visit Piedra de Penol also known as El Penon de Guatape. It was once worshipped by the Tahamies Indians."

It took about two hours to get there, and when the rock first came into view Margie grabbed Matt's arm and pointed. "Matt look, it's amazing!"

The massive ten million ton rock was almost entirely smooth. When they got closer they could see a long crack along one side. When they got even closer they could clearly see the six hundred forty-nine step masonry staircase built into the crack. Alfredo explained that this staircase was the only way to the top. He said he had been to the top and taken pictures from a three-story lookout tower. The view was magnificent, but he explained that the climb was a huge operation. He did not mention Margie's leg. Instead, he pulled out an album of the pictures he had taken. The pictures showed a series of lakes and islands surrounding the rock. In the back of the album, he had pasted old postcards. They showed the view of the area before it was dammed in to create the lakes.

Once they got into Guatape, they understood why Alfredo had referred to it as the most colorful town on earth. Margie went one better and called it the brightest, most cheerful city on earth. The lake area around El Penon was so dramatic that they spent the rest of the day touring it, often walking from little bridge to little bridge to get from one peninsula to the next.

The day flew by and it was evening before they got back to Medellin. Alfredo had one request. La Pampa Parrilla Argentina was known as the best restaurant in Medellin. He had never been there. He carefully suggested they go there for dinner and maybe take him along.

Matt thought it was a great idea. "I love good food, and all that walking has made me hungry. Alfredo, I'll rely on you to help me select something I can't get in the US."

Margie was worried. "We're not dressed for a fancy restaurant."

Alfredo was not about to miss a chance to eat at the famous La Pampa. "Don't worry about that. You look fine, and here in Medellin we love visitors. You'll be welcome just as you are."

Alfredo had not exaggerated; the restaurant was excellent. The food was superb, and the service was outstanding. Maybe because it was obvious Margie and Matt were visitors, or maybe because the young lieutenant was in uniform signifying the visitors were VIP's he was escorting. Either way, the restaurant outdid themselves. Margie, certainly no stranger to nice restaurants, was impressed. "This was the perfect way to cap off two glorious days in Medellin. Alfredo, you have changed the way I used to think about Columbia."

Chapter Thirteen

As he had done the previous evening Matt walked Margie to her room. Margie put the key in the door and said, "Alfredo is a great guy but with him and his soldiers constantly hovering over us it's hard to sit down and relax. Would you like to come in so we can chat for a while?"

Matt had been hoping she would ask and was quick to reply, "I would love to."

Once inside the room Margie offered Matt a drink from the mini-bar. After she poured him a drink, she plopped down on the couch. "I didn't think I'd enjoy Medellin this much. I'm glad we came; I had a great time."

Matt took a long sip from his drink. "Me too. And you made it extra special."

"And what did I do for you to say that?"

"You're just so open to explore and enjoy new things. That's infectious, and it rubs off on me. I love being with you."

Margie was surprised; she did not expect Matt to say something like that. "Matt what are you saying. Are you trying to flatter me?"

"It's just an honest statement. I like being with you."

Margie laughed; she didn't take Matt's words that seriously. "Watch out, you might give an impressible girl like me the wrong idea."

"I'm more serious than you think. I agree, touring Medellin was great, but being with you these last two days made it very special."

Margie stopped laughing. "I have a great time when we do things together, too. I'm really very glad we've become such good friends."

"We could be more than that."

"Oh sure. Matt, come on, me and a guy like you? That won't work. But it's sweet of you to say it. To make me feel good, you're probably willing to tell me you wouldn't mind going to bed with me."

"I wouldn't mind one bit!"

"Matt, stop it. I appreciate your being so nice. Okay, I admit I have a crush on you. What girl wouldn't? But I'm realistic enough to know you would never make love to this mutilated body of mine."

"You're a great person, and I love you a lot, but you have to stop whining about your injuries."

Margie shot to her feet. She was furious. "Whining! I'll show you whining!" In her anger she ripped off her blouse, a type of undershirt she was wearing, and her bra. She spun around and showed Matt her back. "Here's whining!"

Matt looked at her heavily scared back but said nothing. Margie turned around to face him. "You still think anyone would make love to that disgusting mess?"

Matt got up slowly and walked towards Margie. "You have beautiful breasts. And your back, I've seen a lot worse when I was in the military hospital."

"You were wounded?"

"Barely enough to deserve the Purple Heart." He took a few more steps and took her in his arms and kissed her. Then he put his hand under her chin and looked straight into her eyes. "To answer your question; yes, I want to make love to you. Margie, during the last several months I have slowly fallen more and more in love with you. There is no part of your body that's not included in my love."

Margie threw her arms around Matt's neck and they stood silently for a while alternating between kissing and just holding each other tight.

Finally Margie spoke. She was so overcome by emotion that her thoughts came out garbled. "I never believed in miracles. But now that everything I wished for has come true, I'm a believer. Darling, this is a miracle. Anyway, to me it is. After my accident I could only dream of having someone love me. I knew it could never happen to a cripple like me. Certainly not someone like you! You're the kindest, nicest and bravest person in the world, And, I might add, very good looking. You accept me the way I am! What did I do to deserve this?"

"Well, you made me fall in love with you."

Matt's remark made both of them laugh, and they finally let go of each other. Margie had one more hang up she was worried about. "Matt what about my leg?"

"Yes, I know honey. It's also scarred, but so what?"

"It's not the scars I'm worried about. Matt I can't move it. I can't control it. How can I make it nice for you; I can't perform the girl's part."

"I'm sure we'll work it out. Stop worrying"

Margie was already two thirds undressed and Matt started pulling at her slacks. "Hold on I have to take this damn brace off."

"You want me to steady you or do you want to use the chair over there?"

"Then how would I get to the bed? Remember I can't walk on one leg."

"If I remember correctly I carried you before. The distance was a lot longer."

Margie sat down in the chair and pulled her slacks off. She glanced at Matt and he was not sure if she was self-conscious about sitting there wearing nothing but panties or if she was worried about his reaction to her scarred leg, or the brace, or both. Margie carefully placed the brace on the floor next to the chair. "Now that you've seen me naked, it's your turn. Off with the clothes, big boy."

Matt stripped down quickly. Margie wanted him to know she was comfortable with what they were doing. "Wow! That's one hell of a body. I really hit the jackpot. Your scars are a joke compared to mine." She lifted her arms, ready to be lifted. "Having a bad leg might not be all bad. I love being carried by you."

Matt carried Margie to the bed and put her down gently. She pulled off her panties and pulled him on top of her. Matt hugged and kissed her. His hands were all over her body and he did not avoid her back. Margie was still too new at this to do much more than to rub the back of Matt's neck. When Margie's breathing became more rapid and she squeezed his neck so hard it hurt a little, Matt carefully pushed her right leg out of the way as he slowly entered her vagina.

Their bodies were shiny from sweat when Margie sat up and pushed back against the pillows. She had a big grin on her face. "That was marvelous. It was everything I imagined it could be. Was it okay for you?"

Matt snuggled against her chest and grunted what sounded like yes. Margie persisted. "Was it okay, even if I couldn't use my right leg?"

"Honey, that made it better. One less leg to get in my way." As he said it he realized that to Margie it was not a joke. To make sure her handicap would not make her feel less of a woman he continued, "When I moved your leg out of the way I only did it because I was afraid to hurt you when I entered you. After that I completely forgot about your leg. Seriously, it made no difference."

Margie looked down at Matt lying against her chest. "Would you mind staying here with me tonight?"

"I was hoping you'd ask."

Margie slid back down and pushed her good leg over Matt so their bodies were tight against each other. She said a few more endearing words and fell fast asleep. Matt adjusted his body slightly, so he could feel her firm breasts pressing against his chest. It did not take long before he, too, was asleep.

Chapter Fourteen

The next morning Margie was the first to wake up. Her slight move woke-up Matt.

"Oops, look at the clock. I better get back to my room to get ready; Alfredo will be here pretty soon to pick us up."

"We've got plenty of time. He said he'd be here between nine-thirty and ten. We could order breakfast to be brought up to the room. That way you can stay a little longer. Is that okay with you?"

"I'd love it. But I don't have a robe or something to put on. Maybe I'll just pull on my pants.

"No need for that. I saw two bath robes hanging on back of the bathroom door. I'll get them." Margie moved to the edge of the bed; she was trying to get up. As if it was a routine he'd done a thousand times before, Matt got up to get Margie's brace from where it was lying on the floor and brought it to her.

Margie, still naked, put on the brace and headed for the bathroom. Halfway there she turned. "Matt you're very special. You did that like it was the most natural thing in the world. You didn't make me feel like a cripple needing help."

Matt looked at her nude body. "Honey, the one thing that does not come to my mind when I look at your nude body is cripple."

"You're just a sweetheart hiding in Superman's body." She turned around, not afraid to expose her back now, and went to get the bathrobes.

They ordered a huge breakfast which came with lots of fresh fruit and a big plate of fried empanadas. Matt passed on the empanadas. Margie was willing to try, and Matt asked if she liked them. "They're actually quite good. Nice and savory, but little heavy for breakfast."

After they finished breakfast they sat for a while, neither of them willing to end this magical time together. Margie felt confident that Matt was not just being nice, that he really loved her. She finally asked what had been on her mind. "What about Helga. She was so beautiful; do you still think about her?"

"Of course I do."

"After her isn't it difficult to love someone like me?"

"You know if someone besides you would ask me that question I would punch them in the nose. It's insulting to you. Yes, I loved Helga, but with you it is so different."

"I know I'm on thin ice here, but can you explain *different?*"

"That's a hard thing to ask me, but that is precisely what I love about you. Totally open and not afraid of the truth. I already told you; I love being with you. Not that you are a carefree person, far from it. But you're optimistic; enjoy things and fun to be with."

"Before she died, Helga told Maya that you two were very much in love."

"Yes we were. After she killed herself, I thought a lot about our relationship. I discussed it with a psychiatrist who helped me after my breakdown before my trial. She said that our relationship was in part based on our isolated environment in Irbil. We were not integrated in a normal surrounding and it was very much us against the world. The psychiatrist was sure that if we would have returned to a more normal life, Helga's demons would once again get the better of her. Her childhood experience left her deeply scarred. I agreed with her that Helga's childhood experience was deep inside and very hard to erase. But I am sure my love for her helped her conquer her demons. We were deeply in love and there will always be a special place for her in my heart. Your scars are on the surface and I'm not diminishing the affect they have had on you. But you're so different from Helga that my love for you is in no way diminished by my memories of Helga."

"I'm glad you shared that with me. I was afraid I would forever be competing with a woman who was a legend in our company and in your heart. But I have something else I'm worried about. Everything was so great last night that we forgot about protection. My accident did not prevent me from getting pregnant. We could have a problem."

"If I did not intend to marry you, I would not have gone to bed with you."

"Matt what are you saying? Are you proposing?"

"Do you want me to get on my knees to ask?"

"*Matt*, really, really! Do you mean it?"

"You haven't said yes."

"*YES, YES a hundred times yes!*"

Matt went over and kissed her. Cruelly, the phone rang at just that time. It was Alfredo calling from the lobby. "Sorry to be so early. But it's raining and the road back to Betania will be worse than ever."

Matt had picked up the phone. "We'll be down as soon as possible. How long do you think it will take to get back?"

"Maybe an hour extra."

"Okay, please wait in the lobby. Order a coffee and charge it to my room."

Not until he hung up did Matt realize he should have given the phone to Margie. Alfredo would not have expected him to answer Margie's room phone.

Alfredo's warning had been correct. The road was horrible; the washouts were so bad that even the army humvee had trouble getting through. At the power station the rain had caused damage to the equipment and the IEDC crew had to spend an extra four days to finish the job.

Margie did not mind the delay. Matt had moved into her room, and she had a big smile on her face as she supervised the work of her crew. Word of the new sleeping arrangement got back to the home office. Maya called Margie, "Why did I have to hear the good news through the scuttlebutt?"

"Damn it, Maya, I wanted to tell you in person. You heard only half. *We're engaged!*"

"Margie that is terrific. I love you to death and always hoped for the best for you, but this is beyond anything. He's a prince."

"Does Dad know anything?"

"Not yet. Call him right now, so he hears it from you."

Sam was not totally surprised. He had been hoping the two would get together. Seeing Margie light up whenever Matt walked into the room had strengthened his belief that something was brewing. When Margie put Matt on the phone to formally ask Sam for his permission to marry his daughter, Sam roared with laughter. "Why did you two make me wait so long? Hell, I was planning your engagement party before you even knew you'd get engaged."

The big event took place less than a month after Margie and Matt were back in Austin. Sam did not do things in a small way. The engagement party was huge. Everybody he knew was invited. Even Vanessa and Piet Bailey were invited. They respectfully declined.

After they were officially engaged Matt gave up his apartment and moved in with Margie. IEDC continued to successfully sign new orders, and both Margie and Matt spent a lot of their time training new people. Because of their heavy work load, they decided to delay their marriage until the next summer.

However, the baby decided not to wait that long. In her third month Margie developed a prominent baby bump. Sam was much too old fashioned to be happy with a grandchild born out of wedlock. He made no bones about it. He was thrilled to become a grandfather, but he wanted them married before the child was born.

Margie and Matt readily agreed. To show his appreciation for their respect of his wishes, Sam frequently took them shopping to select some of the many wedding presents he wanted to get them. As he did with all things, he relied on Maya's guidance in planning these shopping sprees and frequently asked her to come along.

On a sunny Saturday afternoon, the four of them were walking along Congress Avenue. Sam and Maya were several steps ahead of Margie and Matt. Margie noticed her father holding Maya's hand. She nudged Matt and pointing at it whispered, "What do you think about that?"

Matt smiled and softly said, "Don't know, but it sure looks good. Two buddies out shopping." They giggled, but did not think much further about it.

Late one afternoon during the following month, Sam announced he had seen a beautiful baby cup in a jewelry store half way between the Capitol and Lady Bird Lake. He wanted them to look at it before he bought it for the baby. The four of them took a cab downtown to see the cup.

They all agreed the cup was beautiful; however it was extravagantly expensive. Sam said he didn't care; after all it was for his grandchild. Sam asked the sales lady to put the cup on reserve. "After the baby is born, I'll give you the name and date for engraving. I'm too superstitious to pay for it now but please hold it for us. Do you know about the ring?"

"Of course Mr. Stine. I'll tell the manager you're here."

"Please do. He called to tell me it was ready"

"Yes it is. I saw it. It's really beautiful. They did such great job in setting the two stones. Mr. Stephenson will get it out of the safe for you. One moment please, we'll be right back."

Mr. Stephenson appeared carrying a velvet covered, red box. After greeting Sam and being introduced to Maya,

Margie, and Matt, he carefully opened the box and showed Sam the ring.

Sam was delighted. "Now that's a fine piece of jewelry. Can you take it out of the box so I can hold it?"

The manager carefully pulled the ring from the box and handed it to Sam. Sam held the ring for a moment and pretended he was afraid to drop it. "Oh boy I'm afraid to drop it. Here Maya put it on your finger, so I can admire it."

Maya placed it on her finger. "Yes Sam it's exquisite, but what will you do with it?"

"Give it to you."

"Sam, you're crazy. This ring is much too expensive to give as a gift."

She was about to take the ring from her finger when Sam said, "So, you're turning me down?"

Maya was confused. "Sam, what are you saying? What do you want with this ring?"

"You agree that you like it?"

"Well, ...yes. But, so what?"

"Then agree to marry me, and you can keep it."

Maya was about to keel over and Margie screamed, "Daddy, is this for real?"

Matt somewhat retained his composure, "Maya, say yes. Please, say yes."

Maya stared at the ring. She could not believe what she had just heard. It took a long time before she spoke. "Sam, I've loved you for a long time. Because of you, I've never been serious about another man. No one could measure up to you. Sam, I love you. I'd marry you even without this beautiful ring."

The customers in the store looked up as Margie screamed, "Yes, Yes!" She raced over to Maya hugged her and dragged her over to her father. She was kissing them both and yelling and screaming for joy. Her joy infected the store personnel and the other customers. They all started clapping. Maya was still shaking from emotion.

Matt moved in next to her and gave her arm a comforting squeeze. "Go ahead. After all these years, it's okay to kiss him. Go on. Let that big bear take you in his arms."

Chapter Fifteen

It was one of those lazy Sunday mornings. Margie and Matt were still in bed. The sun drifted in through the large picture window and they admired their bird's eye view of Austin. They knew that once the baby came they would have to give up the one bedroom penthouse Margie had bought the year before she left for Niger. Matt reached over and patted Margie's tummy. "I think I feel the baby moving."

Margie loved it when Matt rubbed her stomach. "Matt, I'm so happy you're his or her dad."

Matt burst out laughing. "Considering we're going to be married in two weeks that's nice. What brought that on?"

"I'm serious Matt. Hug my tummy so our baby can feel secure. I want our child to feel safe, like I did when you picked me up in Niger and held me in your arms. I had been terrified for months, I was sure they would kill me. You held me in your arms and said, 'Hold on we're going home.' I buried my head against your chest and your strength seemed to engulf me. For the first time in months, I felt safe. I had no doubt, we were going home."

Matt responded, "And I want our child to have the same resilience as its mother. To bounce back like you did after the harrowing experience you went through is amazing. Anyone one else would have emerged with some form of PTSD. Shit! I had a slight case of it the first time I came home from Afghanistan. But not you. From the moment you arrived back here in Austin you were the same cheerful, optimistic person you had always been. The person I fell deeply in love with. Besides being terribly sexy, you've got the best personality of anyone I've ever met."

For a moment Margie became sentimental and reached over to kiss Matt. Then she looked at him and smiled, her eyes sparkled when she said, "Okay big shot. I dare you to make love to a fat cripple."

They stayed in bed for a long time after they made love. They were just about to get up when the phone rang. It was Sam. He and Maya had decided to be traditional and not move in together before marriage. "I just called Maya to discuss a few new ideas I have for the wedding. Since the four of us agreed on a double wedding I want to bounce my new ideas off you guys."

His new ideas proved to be very detailed, and Margie was on the phone with her dad for more than half an hour. When she finally hung up she said, "Sorry I took so long. I like most of his ideas, but they are over the top. What he is planning is expensive as hell. I told him maybe we should tone it down a bit. But you know how my dad is. He doesn't just tell you his ideas, he sells them. It's your wedding too, and I want him to consider your input. Dad means well, but he's used to doing things his way, if it's not too crazy, Maya and I have always let him have his way, but I want you to also have a say in what we're planning."

"Sweetheart, I appreciate your concern. Not that our wedding isn't important to me, but I have no specific wishes. Besides, Sam has a lot more experience in planning celebrations than I. From what I have seen so far, he does a terrific job. True, he sometimes goes a little over the top, but he's Sam, and he can get away with it."

Margie had been right. The wedding celebration was over the top. Figuratively and literally. Three huge tents had been erected on the grounds behind the mansion. The guest list was even larger than at the engagement party. The wedding ceremony was planned in the ballroom followed by a reception on the back terrace. A seated dinner was served in two of the tents. The largest of the three tents was set up for desert and dancing. Sam had hired a complete orchestra and also flown in a combo and two popular artists from Nashville.

Above all, Maya and Sam made sure this was Margie's wedding. While Margie had on an elaborate designer wedding dress, Maya was dressed in a flowered evening dress. Matt was dressed in his tuxedo, and Sam was wearing a dark suit.

Sam insisted in walking his daughter from the back of the ballroom through the rows of seated guests, up to the front were the mayor was waiting to perform the ceremony. Matt and his best man Jimmy McDowell were standing on one side of the mayor, and Maya stood on the other side. Margie had asked Maya to be her maid of honor.

In order to give their daughter away as her parents, Sam and Maya took their vows first. When the mayor asked, "Who presents this woman and this man to be married to each other?" In unison, Maya and Sam loudly answered, "We do."

The weather cooperated; it was a beautiful day. After the double ceremony, the guests spilled out of the ballroom onto the terrace. During the reception, Vanessa approached Maya. She was dressed in a red skin-tight dress cut deep in the front and showing most of her back. She still looked every bit like the sexy supermodel who had caught Sam's eye. "Maya, thank you so much for inviting us. We were not quite ready to come to the engagement party, but we want to be friends."

From the big smile on her face Maya could tell she was happy. "I'm so glad you came. I hate it when there are hard feelings. I assure you there are none on our side. As always, you look lovely."

Vanessa laughed. "I'm probably showing a little too much, but Piet loves it when men stare at me. He knows he's got nothing to worry about. I love him to death. With him it's *you can look, but don't dare touch.*"

Maya was pleased. "Vanessa, I'm so glad the two of you are getting along so well. I can tell you're happy. With that smile on your face, you are so beautiful."

Vanessa was carrying a small box. She handed it to Maya, "I've brought you a gift. I would like you to unwrap it."

Maya unwrapped the gift. It was an elegant broach modestly hiding its value. "Vanessa, it's gorgeous!"

"I had it made for you. The diamond in the center is from the engagement ring Sam never asked me to give back. My marriage to Sam was a mistake, and for a time, this diamond was on the wrong finger. Now, I want you to have it. It's where it really belongs. Maya, you have always been so kind and understanding. Even though I was married to the man you loved, you supported me. No one else did. You might not have realized it, but there were times I desperately needed your kind words. At dinners, when Sam ignored me, you'd come up to me and tell me I looked stunning, and you would take me over to introduce me to the guests."

"Vanessa you're very beautiful and the guests, especially the men, loved talking to you. The truth is, Sam was wrong. I love him dearly, but the way he treated you was not right."

"They say, all is well that ends well. Without Sam I would never have met Piet. So, in a way, I have to be grateful. But you're the angel who brought Piet and me together. I love you Maya. You gave me back my world."

Maya gave Vanessa a hug and pinned the broach on her dress. "It will remind me that our dreams came true. I can include Margie's."

"Maya, I have one more favor to ask."

"What's on your mind?"

"Matt has been avoiding me, and I want to speak to him."

Maya took Vanessa by the arm and the two of them went to look for Matt. Matt saw them approach and tried to duck away. Maya was too quick for him and before he got away she said, "Matt I've been talking to Vanessa, and she would like to speak to you. Before I leave you two to talk things over, look at this beautiful broach she gave me."

Vanessa took Matt by the arm and led him away from the crowd so no one could hear what she said. "Hey, don't look so anxious. I've come to apologize. What I did was stupid. No, it was unforgivable. You are an honorable man, and I want to thank you for being so strong. I was deeply depressed, and I was desperate for someone to show me I was still desirable. Ever since I was a young girl, boys and men have always been interested in me. As a model, I had many proposals. Believe it or not, I was still a virgin when I married Sam. Once we were married, Sam lost interest in me, and I lost my self-confidence. You're a super attractive man and I made a terrible mistake. I'm here to apologize and thank you for rejecting me. I behaved like a slut. That's not the real me. You'll laugh when I tell you that at times I've been called a prude."

"Now that you're so honest with me, I have to tell you. You made it very hard for me to resist. I'm not flattering you when I tell you what you offered is what men dream of. If you hadn't been Sam's wife, I would not have walked away."

"Nice of you to say, but I'll echo what most of the guests have already told you. With Margie you've hit the jackpot. We didn't get along while I was married to her father, but she is one hell of a girl."

After the dinner the guests proceeded to the large tent. Margie proved she was a real trouper. She had not attempted to dance since her accident, but she danced the first dance with her father. Her dad knew her limitations and they successfully rounded the dance floor until they switched partners with Maya and Matt. While Sam and Maya proved their skill at ballroom dancing, Matt and Margie did more hugging than dancing.

The festivities lasted until deep into the night. Due to the late hour Margie and Matt decided to stay at the mansion rather than drive back to their apartment. The master suite was on the ground floor and the guest rooms were on the second floor. As they climbed the stairs on the way to their room, Margie said to Matt, "It's strange to see Maya and my dad go into the same bedroom."

Matt smiled, "You better get used to it, honey. Maya is your mom now."

Chapter Sixteen

Margie went into labor several weeks early. She was at the office when the contractions started coming. Sam panicked and Matt was not much better. Maya took control of the situation and called Margie's obstetrician. The doctor's nurse advised her to go to the hospital if the contractions came every ten minutes or less. The doctor was at the hospital and she would let him know that Margie could be coming in.

When the frequency of the contractions reached just under fifteen minutes, Maya decided not to take any chances and told Margie it was time to leave. Even before Maya called the doctor, Matt had already brought his car up front. With Margie in the back seat comforted by Maya, he sped to the hospital. Maya kept admonishing him that slow and safe was better than fast and reckless.

When they arrived, the contractions started coming faster and faster. Margie was rushed to the delivery room. Maya stayed with her and assured her they had plenty of time. She was wrong; in half an hour Margie was holding a healthy baby girl in her arms. "Look Maya, look at her. Isn't she beautiful? Where did she get this blond hair?"

Maya reminded her that her mother had gorgeous blond hair. One of the nurses said, "Don't be surprised if her hair turns darker. A lot of babies have blond hair at birth, but it doesn't always stay." She brought Matt into the room. "Say hello to your baby daughter."

Matt kissed Margie and carefully took the baby's hand. Margie asked what he was doing. "Counting fingers and toes." Both nurses and the doctor burst out laughing. "Don't worry; she's complete. You would have known if you two had agreed to watch the ultra sound."

Maya excused herself and stepped out of the room to call Sam. He was in the hospital's lobby anxiously waited for the call. "Can I come in and see my granddaughter?"

"Sure, where are you?"

"Downstairs in the lobby. You didn't expect me to stay at the office waiting for our first grandchild to be born." Maya went down to the lobby to get Sam. She didn't mention it, but Sam's use of the word *our* made her heart melt.

Chapter Seventeen

The house Matt and Margie were building on a five-acre plot Sam had purchased for them as a wedding present, was not finished. The one bedroom penthouse was not big enough for all the baby equipment. Margie and Matt were planning to rent a larger apartment until their new house was finished. That did not happen. Maya persuaded them for the time being to move in with Sam and her. They could have the second floor of the mansion all to themselves. As an extra attraction, she offered built-in babysitting service.

Everything was perfect. Maybe too perfect. Sam and Maya doted over their grandchild, and Matt and Margie got to build their dream house. The four of them concentrated on their little world, and this came back to bite them.

The baby was one year old and had taken her first steps. Sam tried to teach her to say grandpa and Maya loved playing peek-a-boo with her. They were convinced she was the most brilliant child ever. IEDC was doing well, and work at the office continued at a fast pace. Matt was in his office mapping out the equipment needed for a new project they had contracted for. His cell phone rang; it was Vanessa.

"Hi, Matt, I didn't want to disturb you at work, but I have something important to tell you."

Matt was concerned. "Hi Vanessa. Everything okay? Is Piet all right?"

"Yes, thank you. He's drilling in some God forsaken country. I just spoke to him by phone, and that's what I want to talk to you about."

"What's up?"

"In order not to get his rigs and other equipment wrecked he pays protection money to a high-ranking government official who pockets the money. Last night he had dinner with that official, and the creep got drunk. He boasted about getting money from other companies. Matt, he mentioned IEDC."

"Nonsense, I would know about that."

"Matt hear me out. Here's what Piet told me. IEDC is building a huge power station in the same country where Piet is drilling. Someone in your company is ordering equipment that is not needed. The equipment is intercepted before it reaches your building site, and this government guy sells it."

"Why in the hell would we do that? In all the countries we work the government guarantees protection. They reimburse us if any equipment is damaged due to local violence. We wouldn't accept the job if it wasn't for that. We can't risk a local rebellion."

"The guy told Piet someone on your end gets a kickback for cooperating in this scheme."

"Did Piet tell who?"

"No, but I can ask him."

"Please do. Find out what he's heard, but don't tell anyone but me. Sam would die if he heard someone in his company was on the take."

"I understand, Piet is the same way."

Two days later Vanessa called, "Matt I'm sorry to have to tell you, it's Aleksy Dubinski." The name hit Matt like a punch in the gut that knocked him over. "Hey Matt, Matt, are you still there?"

"Yes, Vanessa, I'm still here. Are you sure? How did Piet get this information?"

"He told the guy he was bluffing, just trying to collect more protection money, but the guy offered more details. I'm so sorry Matt. Piet is devastated. He likes Aleksy, and he'd give anything not to have to tell you this."

After Matt hung up he sat silently at his desk. He was dazed and did not know what to do. Vanessa's words 'it's Aleksy' kept ringing in his ear. Tears where running down his face and he pounded his desk with both fists.

Then he heard Maya's voice *we here at IRDC have your back no matter what. We're on your side.*

He got up and walked over to Aleksy's office and went in. Without saying a word he closed the door behind him and sat down. Aleksy looked up from the papers that where spread out on his desk. "You have some thing for me, Matt?"

Matt responded softly, "I'm having a nightmare. I hope you can tell me it's just a dream, so the horrible information I got is not real."

Aleksy did not think Matt was serious. "What the hell is that all about?"

"Tell me about the rumor you purchased superfluous equipment."

Aleksy froze. He was about to respond but stopped. He did not look at Matt when he finally spoke. "Will you let me leave the company quietly without pressing charges? Does Sam know?"

Aleksy was not looking at him, but Matt shook his head no. "Nobody knows but me."

Aleksy grabbed some personal items and started for the door. Matt stopped him. "You, of all people! Aleksy, we're friends. The least you owe me is an explanation. In heaven's name why?"

"I had no choice. They were about to foreclose on my house."

"How is that possible? You earn a great salary."

"Not enough to pay all the medical bills."

"What bills? We've got great insurance here at the company."

"Yes, but that did not help."

"What happened? Didn't the insurance pay for your son Alec's medical bills?"

"Yes but Alec had ALS. All his medical bills were covered. His younger brother Benny had an incurable brain tumor. All his treatment was experimental, not covered by insurance."

"Why didn't we know about that?"

"When our eldest son Alec died four years ago. Caitlin took it very hard. You were there, you know. Margie and everyone did everything possible to support us, but Caitlin was inconsolable. Then, when our Benny was diagnosed with a brain tumor, she went into denial. No matter what the doctors said, she believed he could be cured. She went so far as to refuse to tell anybody what was wrong with Benny. When she heard about an experimental treatment, I could not deny her this remote chance to save our boy. The cost was unbelievable, and as I said, insurance does not pay for experiments. We went through our savings in a hurry. I was forced to mortgage our home. As you know, Benny died two years ago but I've been unsuccessful in paying off our bills."

"Why the hell didn't you come to us? We would have helped."

"Sure, can you hear me tell Sam, 'I need some money to pay off some quack doctors for a cure I have been told won't work.' "

Matt got up and put his arms around Aleksy. He had tears in his eyes. "Damn it, I'm your fucking friend. Yes, you could have told me. How much do you owe?"

"I still owe them about two hundred thousand dollars."

"That's all? We can fix that."

"That's not the whole story."

"Okay out with it. We're going to fix this! Tell me from the beginning how we got here."

"The doctors at some of the best clinics in the country told us there was nothing they could do for Ben. Then Caitlin read about this treatment, and we agreed to try it. I knew chances were just about zero that we could save Ben. I love my wife. I could not tell her I would let her one remaining child die without trying everything to save him. The treatment center billed us for incredible amounts. As I told you, when our savings ran out I mortgaged our house, but we still owed a substantial sum of money. For the last two years I have been paying down the remaining debt, but a few months ago they demanded fifty thousand dollars, or they would go after our house. I was maxed out on all my credit cards and with our heavy mortgage there was no way we could borrow more money. I could think of only one way to get my hands on the fifty thousand the clinic demanded. It is common knowledge that in the country where we're building this huge hydroelectric power station, the government officials are on the take. Matt, I contacted them and made the deal. Now, I could shoot myself for it."

Matt had fully recovered. "Nah, we don't want blood all over this office."

"Will you let me resign without anyone else knowing what I did?"

"No! That is, no, I won't let you resign. Look, I was once stupid enough to think I was doomed because there was nobody to help me. Wrong! Now you need a little help. You have been a terrific friend for me and you have to allow me to help. Allow, no, I *demand* the right to help. Go home. Give Caitlin a big hug for me and tell her I've missed her terribly at our parties the last several years. Now I finally understand. Margie and I will be over later this evening and we will come up with a plan to solve all of this."

Chapter Eighteen

Matt felt he had to tell Margie about Aleksy. Even though it very much involved the company, he was sure she would agree her father should be spared from hearing about Aleksey's troubles until all the dust was settled. Matt knew Sam would never forgive himself for not being aware of the heartache Aleksy and his wife had gone through. Sam would hate himself for not stepping in and helping both financially and emotionally. But Margie should be told. If Matt wanted to help Aleksy financially, he had to use some of their personal finances, and he could not very well do that without consulting her. However, what weighed heaviest on his decision to involve Margie was that he could not imagine keeping a secret from her.

He told her the full story and asked, "Margie, are you angry about what he did."

"I'm shocked, deeply shocked, but angry no. If I'm angry, it's at us. How could we be so selfish as to let this happen? It's not like the Dubinskis are some distant acquaintances living in a far of land. They're part of us, part of our company, and we failed them. I feel horrible about this; we've been behaving like a set of self-centered brats. Is that what happens to rich kids? Are we too spoiled to really care about others?"

Matt agreed with her. "You're right. They lost both their sons in the space of four years, and we stood on the sidelines. When Aleksy told me the full story I was just about in tears. You're right. How could I let this happened to a man who's done so much for me? If you agree, I have an idea how to make it right. Here's what I'd like us to do . . ."

Without any hesitation, Margie agreed to Matt's proposal. "I know where the Dubinskis do their banking. I'll call the manager right now and tell him we're coming to see him."

It was around dinner time when Margie and Matt pulled into the driveway of the Dubinskis' rustic home. They were loaded down with lots of food they had picked up on the way. Caitlin came out to greet them, and when Margie stepped out of the car she got a big bear hug. "Margie, I'm so glad to see you. Sorry I kept away so long." Margie made it very clear she should have been the one to come by and see Caitlin.

Aleksy helped Matt bring the food in. Margie helped Caitlin set the table, but before they sat down to dinner Matt had an announcement. "Earlier this evening we stopped by your bank. The bank manager was very accommodating, and we took the liberty of paying off your mortgage."

Before either Aleksy or Caitlin could say a word, Matt continued. "While we were there we also handed him a check for two hundred thousand dollars to be deposited in your account."

Now it was Aleksy's turn to start crying. "Too much! Too much! You did not have to do that. That's much too much!"

Caitlin wound up in Margie's arms. "How did you know they we're going to take our house?"

Margie had no idea how much Caitlin knew, "A little birdy told us. The birdy also told us to shape up and take care of our friends."

Aleksy reached out with both hands to Matt. "Matt, seriously, this is too much. Why so much? I don't know if we can accept that."

"I'll tell you why. Margie and I are too stinking rich to know what it is like to be haunted by unpaid bills. We did not deserve all the dough we got, and you two certainly did not deserve what happened to you. So, it evens out."

Aleksy looked at Caitlin and again burst out in tears. Caitlin looked over at him. "What's the matter, sweetheart. You're crying. Aren't you happy?"

"Darling, happy can't describe it. This is the first time I've seen you smile since Alec passed away."

The food Margie and Matt brought was hardly touched. They had carefully selected things everybody would like, but emotions ran too high for any of them to eat much. They sat around and talked for a long time, and Margie and Matt did not get home till well after midnight.

Before Margie fell asleep she said. "Matt, I feel so good about what we did for those two wonderful people. To see the love in that man's eyes when he saw his wife's smile was worth every penny."

Chapter Nineteen

A formal looking envelope arrived in the mail. It was addressed to Lieutenant Colonel Matthaeus Ramsey, retired. *That's odd,* Margie thought. She turned the envelope over. In embossed letters, it read Headquarters United States Army, Washington, DC. Matt wasn't home yet, so she put it aside for him. When she heard him come in she called out to him, "A formal looking letter from the army came for you. I wonder what that's all about. I've put it on the dining room table."

"Probably nothing much. I'm through with them. You can go ahead and toss it."

"If you don't what to, I'll see what they want." Margie retrieved the letter.

"Hey, how about this! A four-star general wants to come see you. It says he's retired, but still, I've never met a four-star general before. That's pretty darn exciting."

"Do they give his name?"

"Yes they do. It's General Edelman. Do you know him?"

"Yeah I know him. We'll tell him not to come. I don't want to see him."

"Why on earth not?"

"When I needed him, he was not there for me, and I don't need him now."

"He abandoned your unit in battle or what?"

"He's the one who arrested me."

"Is he the one who brought those false charges against you?"

"Nah, he just carried out orders. But he should have known I could not have done what they charged me with. He knew me. He should have known better and stood up for me. I don't want to see him!"

"Matt, that's not like you. He carried out orders. Maybe he should have helped you. But that's no reason, after all these years, to carry a grudge. That's not at all like the Matt I married."

Matt kept grumbling about it, but Margie insisted. He had to respond to the letter and let them know he would be happy to receive the general.

Two weeks later, exactly on the agreed time, Margie saw three large black SUVs come up the driveway. "Looks like more than a visit; it's an invasion."

Three men stepped out of the middle SUV, two wore business suits but the third man was in full military dress. Matt met the men at the door, and immediately recognized General Edelman. One of the other men also looked familiar. Matt was sure he knew him, but couldn't quite place him. The man helped him remember. He stuck out his hand and said, "Yes, I'm Leo the guy you pulled out of that burning Apache. A little less bloody than the last time you saw me and in a lot better shape. And dressed in that beautiful uniform is Brigadier General Carpenter. To me, he's still just plane Daniel the other guy you dragged out of the chopper. He only got to outrank me because I retired."

General Edelman introduced himself and the other two men to Margie. She had not expected the men to be so informal, and was relieved she didn't have to follow army etiquette which she was not familiar with. When General

Edelman explained the purpose of their visit, she was very grateful she had not discarded the letter.

The general explained that after he retired, he had researched Matt's army career. The whole affair around the false accusation and trial still bothered him. He wanted to know if there was anything the army could have done to prevent a perfectly innocent officer from being charged with such a serious crime. He learned Matt had been awarded the Distinguished Service Cross. He never knew that because Matt only wore fatigues when he came to Baghdad to see him. He never wore any decorations while embedded with the Kurds. When he read the citation that came with the award, he felt it lacked detail. He contacted Daniel who had recently been promoted to Brigadier General and was stationed in the Pentagon. Together they decided to interview everybody involved. The dossier grew thicker and thicker. They managed to trace down everyone. Even the crews of the helicopters that had eventually come to rescue the three of them.

Hand carried by a retired general, the dossier got to the right people in a hurry.

General Edelman paused and motioned for Leo and Daniel to come stand next to him. He stood up and said, "Matt it's our great honor to inform you that the president of the United States invites you to the White House to receive the Congressional Medal of Honor."

Margie let out a piecing scream while the three men saluted the recipient of the Medal of Honor.

ABOUT THE AUTHOR

His family fled the Netherlands shortly after the Nazi invasion. During that time, most countries did not accept refugees, and they passed through half a dozen countries before settling in Curacao and later in Aruba. They immigrated to the United States in 1952. He is a graduate of Washington & Lee University and the NYU School of Law. After law school he joined a law firm in New York City. At Washington and Lee he was enrolled in the R.O.T.C program and he was called to active duty in 1964. He served in the US Army in Germany, retiring as a captain after his tour of duty was completed. The Secretary of the Army awarded him The Army Commendation Medal for his service. He took an overseas discharge and lived and worked in the Netherlands for many years. On returning to the United States, he joined the US subsidiary of a Chinese company. He has lived and worked on four different continents. He is retired and lives in Michigan with his wife, Jan. He has two daughters, five wonderful grandchildren, and two great sons-in-law. Since retiring, he has published six novels.

Author with one of his pals.

Books by Harold J. Fischel

Anthony

ISBN:1494851210

ISBN:13:9781494851217

Taylor, The Journey Home

ISBN:0692341811

ISBN:13:9780692341810

Never Too Late

ISBN:0692404694

ISBN:13:9780692404690

Do No Evil

ISBN:069269210X

ISBN:13:9780692692103

SCARECROW-MORPHED

ISBN: 978-1-54393-119-8 (print)

ISBN:978-1-54393-120-4 (ebook)